# The Titanic Game

# The Titanic Game

## by Mike Warner

all about kids
publishing

Editor:  Robert W. Armstrong

Library of Congress Cataloging-in-Publication Date

LCCN: 2004015079

Warner, Mike
The Titanic Game/by Mike Warner; cover illustrations by Frank Ordaz.
-1st Edition
p.                                                cm.
Summary:  Fifth-grader Dane Sheridan, opposed to his new foster sister, Abby, learns a lesson
in brotherly love when a magic book transports the two back to the Titanic and Dane must save
them both from disaster.

ISBN 978-0-9744446-2-8  0-9744446-2-6

[1. Titanic (Steamship)—Fiction. 2. Brothers and sisters—Fiction. 3. Magic—
Fiction. 4. Books and reading—Fiction. 5. Space and time—Fiction. 6. Foster home care—
Fiction.]

PZ7.W2457 Ti 2005
[Fic] 22  lcac

All About Kids Publishing is a registered trademark.
Printed in the United States of America

All About Kids Publishing
9333 Benbow Drive
Gilroy, CA 95020
www.aakp.com

For my wife Ann, who wouldn't have gotten
on a lifeboat without me.

*Acknowledgements*

Thanks to Mom for reading early drafts of the
manuscript, and to all of my family for their support.

A Titanic thanks to Kerri Atter, the director of the
Molly Brown House Museum, and her wonderful staff,
for all of their help.

Also a special thank you to my former seventh-grade
English teacher and author, Will Hobbs,
for his inspiration and encouragement.

# CHAPTER ONE

Dane Sheridan stood on the blacktop of Silver Rush Elementary, hands jammed into the pockets of his jeans. He was leaning against the red brick building, the gentle early morning September wind blowing its way across the schoolyard and ruffling his sandy blonde hair. His backpack hung sloppily from one jean-jacketed shoulder as he surveyed the usual before school ritual.

Kids getting out of cars.

Kids trudging wearily towards the playground to wait for the bell and the start of the school day.

Kids playing on monkey bars and other pieces of assorted playground equipment.

Kids chasing each other, running off valuable calories gained from breakfast.

Often he was with them and joining in, but he just hadn't felt much like participating lately, and was more in favor of keeping the school wall company. His mood was dark, resembling the gray clouds he could see lazily trekking their way in from the west, being urged on by the wind.

There might be a storm later.

His eyes tracked the reason for his foul mood as she made her way from the sidewalk and entered the gap in the fence and approached the primary playground.

His sister.

Or rather, his foster sister.

Abby Walsh was the reason he had gone from being, as his teacher Mrs. Magruder would say, "a perfectly happy boy," to "a boy with a fierce need for an attitude adjustment." At least that was what she had told him yesterday when she had grilled him on why his behavior had gone screaming downhill like a fiery car crash.

He hadn't answered, only shrugged, which had become his main form of communication lately.

Dane's mom and dad had taken the second grader in a few weeks ago, wanting to give foster parenting a try, even though he had protested strongly. They had told him that it might not be permanent and that she might not end up with them forever, but that they should all try hard and give it a shot.

But he didn't want to give it a shot. He definitely hoped that this wouldn't be permanent. He *liked* being the only child.

*Well, had liked.*

Abby glanced up and saw her brother, her maybe brother, by himself against the school wall. He hadn't walked with her again, and instead left early so he wouldn't have to spend time with her. Sadly she raised an arm to him in a wave in the hopes that he would wave back, but he didn't. He just stood there, propped up against the wall, scowling at her. She dropped her arm and kept moving.

Dane felt a pang of remorse as, with her head down, Abby pushed on against the wind and headed for her playground, her brown hair flowing behind her. He quickly buried his feelings. At this rate, if he continued to be unkind to her, she might not want to stay with them, and then it would be life back to normal.

As the bell that signaled the beginning of the school day rang, Dane pushed himself off the wall and headed for the school entrance. As he walked he was surprised to see the principal, Mr. Hill, looking sternly at him with his arms crossed and standing near the door.

Dane started to walk into the school, but the principal of Silver Rush Elementary raised his arm in Dane's way, blocking his path.

"That was rather rude of you, don't you think, Mr. Sheridan?"

Dane looked at his shoes and shrugged. In some cases

silence was best. He tugged nervously at his white T-shirt.

Mr. Hill stared hard at Dane. When he spoke, displeasure oozed from his voice. "What's gotten into you? That's about the third time I've seen you treat your sister badly since she began her term at this school."

"She's not my sister, just some girl!" Dane shot back, surprising himself. He had never argued with a teacher before. As soon as the words had slipped from his mouth, he knew he was in for it.

Students passed by principal and troublemaker through the entrance as Mr. Hill raised his voice. "I don't care if she's your sister, foster sister, or cousin twice removed. Your parents have taken her in as a service to her and the state of Colorado. For the moment, anyway, that makes her your sister, and on my playground and in my school, you will treat her with respect as you would a real sister."

Dane desperately wanted to ask him if he was finished, but he knew it would only make matters worse.

So he kept his mouth shut.

"The next time I see you treat her like that," Mr. Hill continued, "you and I will have a little talk. No detention, no being sent out into the hall, just straight to my office."

Dane shuddered inwardly. He had heard about Mr. Hill's office before. He was a very effective principal when it came to disciplining his students. Dane had never heard anything really specific, just that it was a place you didn't want to go. Students always came away from the principal's office much better behaved than when they went in.

Mr. Hill lowered his arm. "Try a little harder, okay?" he asked. The menacing tone had left his voice, and he smiled at Dane. "I know you can do better."

Dane nodded and slipped quickly by the principal, glad to be out of the way of the firing squad. As he walked to his classroom he scoffed at what had just transpired. What did the principal know of his situation? Had he ever been in Dane's shoes? One moment he was the one and only child, the next moment he was not able to go anywhere in his own house without a second grade tag-a-long. Dane didn't think so.

He entered his fifth grade classroom and all thoughts of Mr. Hill and his foster sister exited his mind.

For the time being, anyway.

At lunch recess Dane continued his morning activity of doing a whole lot of nothing, along with his two best friends, Kyle and Michael. On occasion they played football or soccer, but on this gray and depressing Thursday they opted to hang around the schoolyard and watch the younger kids chase each other.

"Why do we have to share our lunch recess time with the little kids?" Kyle observed, giving a rock a kick and watching it tumble.

Dane shrugged as Michael said, "Yeah, it means you have to see you-know-who, Dane."

"I don't care," Dane mumbled. "It makes no difference to me."

"Sure," Michael retorted. "We know how you feel about her."

"Don't look now, Dane, but here comes your sister!" Kyle called out, pointing.

"Shut up," Dane stepped back as he watched the little girl walking towards them. "She's not my sister." He jammed his hands further into his pockets, far enough to touch his toes.

"But I thought—"

Kyle argued, but was cut off.

"My parents haven't adopted her," Dane said. "Yet," he added miserably.

"Do they want to?" Michael asked.

"I guess so, but I think they're waiting to see how we get along together."

"Which doesn't seem too good," Kyle observed.

"Well, how well do you two get along with your little sisters?" Dane fired back.

Michael shrugged. "I don't know. I kind of like my sister."

Dane rolled his eyes.

When Abby reached the small group she tentatively

held out her hand, which was stuffed with a wrinkled piece of paper. "I made it in art today for you, Dane," she said proudly.

Dane stared at the piece of construction paper, complete with real leaves waxed onto it. It looked pretty cool, but he wasn't going to let her know he actually thought that.

"Neat," Michael said appreciatively.

Dane scowled. "It looks like a mud puddle," he said unkindly. "What do you think, Kyle?"

"Well, I think it's sort of cool—"

"Shut up, Kyle," Dane cried. Then, to Abby, "Aren't you supposed to be on *your* side of the playground? Beat it. You're taking up my space."

Abby dropped the picture to her side dejectedly and lowered her head as tears welled up in her eyes. She turned from the three and walked to her own area, her red coat blowing behind her in the gentle gust.

"What's gotten into you lately? That was cold," Michael said.

"Yeah," Dane agreed as he watched the retreating figure. "That's what the principal said." He felt a stab of guilt. Was he really that mean? He would have said no a few weeks ago, but now he wasn't so sure. His parents had said that he was possessive of his territory and unwilling to change the way he had lived for ten years. He suspected this was true in that the nest he had ruled ever since he could remember he now had to share with someone he had only known for three weeks. Why shouldn't he feel resentful?

"Cold," he repeated.

Their trio was broken up as the end of lunch recess whistle blew. Michael and Kyle ran across the playground to their class line, but Dane, who didn't feel like running, sulked while walking to join them. On a whim he turned to see where Abby was. She was nearing her own line. As she approached it, two-second grade classmates who met her, blocked her way. Even though he wasn't close to her, he could still catch the conversation.

"Hey, Abby," one of the boys said in a mocking tone. "Why did you bring your art out here?"

The little girl shrugged as she said, "I wanted to show my brother."

*Oh, shut up*, Dane thought. *I'm not your brother.*

"If you bring your art out here, it might get taken," the other boy remarked. As he said this, he lunged forward and seized the project. "Like that!" he said.

"Give that back!" Abby shrieked as she flailed and jumped while making a futile attempt to grab the paper.

The boy held it triumphantly in the air, waving it around as though it were some trophy he was proud to have earned. "I don't think so," he teased.

Dane stepped forward automatically, and then stopped

cold. What was he doing? He didn't care, did he? If he were to help her, she'd really get attached to him, and then he'd never get rid of her. Even though his feet told him to go, to go and do what was right, he just couldn't.

So he continued his walk to his line, still fighting the urge to tell the little second grade creeps to bug off.

Then he looked at her again, once more. Her eyes met his, imploring him for his help, pleading for him to come and get the art back, to assist.

He turned and kept walking, his face growing hot and red.

"Now that was *really* cold," Michael grumbled to Dane when he arrived in the line.

"Well, why didn't you do something, then?" Dane retorted sharply.

"I was too busy watching what you were doing. Or not doing, I guess."

Dane glared at him.

"Principal's out," Kyle observed.

Dane looked up to see that Mr. Hill had indeed arrived and was talking sternly to the two second-graders. He had retrieved Abby's artwork and now held it in his hand as he reprimanded them, his solemn eyes boring holes into the boys, whose heads were hanging down.

And then the principal raised his head and made eye contact with Dane, as if he knew Dane was watching, had known the whole time.

Dane gasped.

The principal slowly shook his head.

# CHAPTER TWO

Dane wasn't surprised when Mrs. Magruder, his teacher, laid a hand on his shoulder and informed him Mr. Hill wanted to see him right away. All the same, he could feel butterflies fluttering about in the pit of his stomach as he exited the room and walked down the hall to the principal's office.

*This is not going to go well*, he thought.

He had heard stories about the principal's office, but how bad could this really be? There was only so much a principal could do to punish a student. Corporal punishment was out these days, thank God. No more beating on kids in school, whether they deserved it or not.

What was Mr. Hill going to do, exile him into the desert?

He told the secretary, Mrs. Sherman, that he was there to see Mr. Hill. She pointed gravely to his office. *Just like the ghost of Christmas future pointed to Scrooge's gravestone,* Dane thought dismally. Boy, was he really in for it, and he hadn't even done anything *that* bad, had he?

The door was open and Dane sauntered in, trying his best to look at ease, but the butterflies were still at work, bouncing off the walls of his stomach.

Mr. Hill was at one of the three bookcases that lined the walls of his office. Dane saw him pull a book from it and set it on the desk behind a stack of papers. He motioned for Dane to take a seat in one of the three chairs across from his desk. As Dane sat, so did the principal.

"I would ask you what you have to say for yourself, but I'm assuming you wouldn't have much to say. Am I right?" The principal folded his hands on his desk and stared at Dane.

Dane remained silent, at a loss from such a beginning. He hated it when teachers and principals played mind games.

"It figures," Mr. Hill said. He continued, "I'm very disappointed in your behavior at lunch recess half an hour ago."

"What did I do?" Dane asked, trying to look helpless in his attempt to play dumb.

"Nothing," the principal shot back. "Absolutely nothing. Two boys were teasing your sister, and you just stood there and watched. Frightened, were you?"

"No!" Dane felt his face going red as the butterflies in his stomach were now rocketing about, slamming into each other and doing flip-flops. Mr. Hill smiled at him, probably amused by the way Dane had blurted out his response. His "no" had sounded more like "Noah," as in the man with the ark.

"But you did nothing!" the principal replied loudly, yet calmly, the little smile still in place on his lips. "Are you trying to make her miserable? It looks like you are certainly succeeding!"

"I don't like her—" Dane started.

"You hardly even know her! What you don't like is having someone move in on your happy home, am I right?"

"I guess," Dane conceded wearily, looking at his hands as he clenched and unclenched them in his lap. But he didn't guess. The principal was right.

"During the past few weeks I have seen you ignore her." Mr. Hill continued. "I have seen you not stick up for her. I've seen you emotionally push her away. And it's not like she's older than you are. She's only in second grade! She can't defend herself very well yet."

Dane sat quietly, waiting for the tirade to end. He wondered briefly what his punishment would be for whatever it was that he had done. How do you write a note home about this? Dear Mr. And Mrs. Sheridan, your son walked away from his sister today...

"I asked your teacher to tell me some of your interests. She said you like the *Titanic*. Is that correct?" Mr. Hill asked.

Dane, shaken from his punishment thoughts, glanced up at Mr. Hill. "Huh?" he said, wondering where the previous conversation had gone. One moment he was being tongue-lashed by Mr. Hill and the next moment the principal wanted to talk about sunken ships.

"You even wrote a report about it," Mr. Hill resumed. From the pile of papers on his desk he produced a ten-page computer-typed report Dane had completed a week and a half ago. He had received an A minus on it, of which his parents (and he) had been extremely proud.

*This is what this is all about?* Dane thought, as it dawned on him that he might just have to write a report for his punishment. Oh well, he could think of worse things.

The principal pushed it forward on his desk to Dane. "I read it. It's very good. You showed a good deal of knowledge about the ship. Not just of the events that took place, but of the ship itself. Very impressive."

Dane waited, curious to see where this was going. He wouldn't necessarily mind doing another report on the *Titanic...*

Mr. Hill stood and handed Dane the book he had taken off the shelf when Dane had first walked in. Dane took the book (bigger than a normal size paperback but smaller than a full blown hardback) and observed the glossy cover, which was slick, new and colorful. The book hadn't been read much, if at all.

*"The Life and Death of the Titanic,"* Dane read. The letters were red and capitalized and had been placed in the sky, just over a watercolor illustration of the ship cutting through the waves on a sunny day. Underneath the picture was a subtitle. *"Disaster on a Grand Scale,"* he breathed.

He had never seen this book before, even though he had gone to the public library and used six or seven books for his report.

"Your knowledge of the ship should help you, as well as this book," Mr. Hill said as he came around the front of the desk and leaned on it near Dane, his arms folded over his chest.

"Help me with what?" Dane asked curiously. Maybe now he would get the answer to this strange session.

"What you need is a game," the principal said, dodging Dane's query.

"This is a book," Dane said, trying not to sound sarcastic. That would only make things worse, but it was a book. What game was Mr. Hill referring to?

But the principal ignored him. "Do you know what the word titanic means?"

Dane hardly needed to think. "Big?"

"That's right," the principal said, giving Dane another

smile. It was a genuine one, this time. "What you need is a big game–a titanic game. That will help straighten you out. Different students need different lessons. You need this one. Everyone can learn from playing a game."

"But what do I do?" Dane asked, confused. He had no clue where this was going, and he felt the principal was being rather cryptic.

"You'll see," he said as he smiled and ushered Dane out of his chair and over to the door. "You'll be starting it this very evening, I believe."

"Start what? I don't even know what you want me to do."

The principal's smile turned cold. "You'll figure it out. You're a smart boy. You will know what to do when the time comes." He virtually pushed Dane out the office door. "And don't lose the book," he offered.

"I won't."

"And good luck."

"What?" He turned.

But the door had snapped shut behind him. The meeting was concluded.

*Good luck?* Dane thought. *That's weird.*

Clutching the book tightly (it wouldn't be prudent to lose one of the principal's books), he left the school office and made his way back to class, feeling lucky and unlucky at the same time. On one hand he was glad he didn't have to do detention or anything. On the other hand he hadn't heard about someone getting into trouble and having to do schoolwork. And shouldn't he have to do a report that pertained to what he had done wrong? What did the *Titanic* have to do with anything?

Weird. Again.

And what exactly had he done wrong anyway? Not played Superman to some girl he hardly knew? It wasn't as if he had thrown bricks through the school window or something. What did his parents and the principal expect from him? That he should have a tea party with her? He just wanted to be left alone.

Arriving at his classroom he entered and for the time being all thoughts of Mr. Hill and his sister left his mind.

# CHAPTER THREE

"Dane! Dinner!"

Dane's mom's voice floated upstairs, interrupting his video game revelry. He snapped off the game system and the TV (his parents hadn't been sure if they wanted him to have one in his room, but he had talked them into it), and pounded down the stairs.

He was famished.

He often walked to the convenience store on his way home from school to get a snack but hadn't done so today. The storm that he had seen approaching this morning had, by three o'clock, become a full-blown electrical show, complete with rain, flashing lights and thunderous claps of noise. It was now six-thirty, but the storm still raged harder than ever, loud enough to make Zelda, his pug dog, quiver nervously on his bed.

"Great Dane!" his dad called cheerfully in greeting as

he entered the dining room. Dane flinched at the nickname his dad had called him since as long as he could remember. It was cute at first, but was now getting old. After all, he was ten, soon to be eleven. He would have to have a talk with Dad before too long.

But not tonight. It was spaghetti night. Nickname talks could wait.

"Hi, Dad," he replied as he sat down with his mom and dad at the table set for four. He didn't ask where *she* was; figuring Abby was probably at a friend's house, if she had any friends. She was probably running late. He usually didn't keep track of his foster sister's limited schedule.

"So, how was school?" his mom inquired.

"Fine." Dane said, taking a bite of spaghetti.

"What did you do today?" his dad asked.

"Nothing."

"Nothing?" his dad pressed, not believing.

"No."

"How is Mrs. Magruder?" his mom said, trying a new subject.

"Okay."

"Did you get into any trouble at school today?" Mom. Jokingly.

"No." Dane. Lying.

Nathan Sheridan stared at his wife. "I love these stimulating dinnertime conversations, don't you, dear?"

The doorbell rang then. Dane grumbled, "There she is," through a mouthful of spaghetti.

"Oh, come now," his mom protested. "You've been getting along with her better lately, haven't you?"

Dane only shrugged.

His dad excused himself and went to the door. He flung it open and grandly exclaimed, "Aunt Betty!"

Dane almost choked on his mouthful. "Aunt Betty?" he asked his mom.

"Yes. Didn't I tell you she was coming?"

"No! I thought..."

"How's my little Daney Waney?" his Aunt Betty screamed as she charged her sizable bulk across the room, water pouring off of her in small waterfalls. She hugged Dane so hard he belched accidentally.

"Fine," Dane wheezed, dripping. Aunt Betty was his dad's older sister. Mom often called her eccentric, whatever that meant. Sometimes her loud ways and boisterous attitude rubbed him the wrong way, and this was one of those times.

Aunt Betty's handbag hit him in the face as she leaned across the square table to hug his mom.

"Sorry I'm late," she apologized loudly. "I had to drive slow because of the storm."

"So, where's Abby?" Dane finally forced himself to ask. He tried to use his best "So has anyone seen my shoes?"

type of voice.

His dad stared hard at Dane now. "Since when did you start caring? You don't even like her. You've been ignoring her ever since we got her."

If Dane had been chewing now he would have choked again at his father's bluntness. Nathan Sheridan didn't often have a rude word to say to anyone, especially not his own son.

"What?" Dane managed.

"She's in her room." His dad sat down and began to eat as Aunt Betty plopped her large behind in the empty chair Dane had assumed had been for Abby. The immense woman dropped her colossal suitcase of a purse on the floor and began helping herself from the dish of spaghetti, all the while babbling to his mom about something. He wasn't sure what. He wasn't listening.

"Upstairs?" he asked his dad.

"Yes, in her room. Where we always keep her."

"Always keep her?" Dane repeated, incredulous. That was a strange term to use when talking about a child, especially when it was coming from his father. An odd and unwelcome feeling began to creep its way into Dane's mind. Did this have something to do with the principal?

His father looked at him impatiently. "Go see for yourself, Dane."

Dane stood, trying to act like everything was normal,

trying not to look alarmed or awkward. He backed away from the table, pushed in his chair, and made himself walk to the stairs. Once out of sight he tore up them, at the same time trying to push away that uneasy feeling.

Everything was fine, right?

Reaching the room that his parents had converted from a junk room into a place for Abby, he flung the door open and flicked on the light.

A birdcage sat on a table in the middle of the room; a bird perched on a branch was inside. Where Abby's bed had been now sat a desk, heaped high with papers and various pieces of bric-a-brac. Around the room sat boxes piled on top of each other, haphazardly strewn about in a disorderly fashion.

The junk room had returned.

"Dane," the bird squawked, making him jump out of his skin.

"Abby?" Dane called out to the room, knowing deep down inside that she wasn't there. Was this what his dad had been talking about? They didn't own a parrot!

"Not your Abby!" the bird shrieked, its green and red head bobbing like one of those dolls you could get at a sporting event. "Your Abby gone!"

Dane gasped, staring.

"There's Abby. Right where we always keep her," his dad said from behind Dane, startling him and making him jump all over again.

Dane turned and his father set his hands on his shoulders. "Are you feeling all right tonight? You don't look very good."

He nodded dumbly. "Fine," he lied.

"Okay," his dad replied. "Just checking. You're looking kind of pasty."

"I'm okay. Just kind of tired, that's all."

"If you're sure, I'm going back to dinner. I have to entertain your Aunt Betty, you know," his father said with a grin.

Dane smiled weakly. "Yeah," he said as his dad turned to leave. Then, stepping out on a limb, he decided to ask the dreaded question that had been creeping up on him since the appearance of Aunt Betty.

"Dad?"

His father turned. "Yes?"

"I don't have a foster sister, do I?"

Nathan laid a hand on his son's forehead, touching his sweaty brow with its mop of sandy blonde hair. "You are kind of warm, but not too hot—"

"Do I, Dad?"

Nathan Sheridan frowned at his son. "Well, not yet. We are thinking about it. You know that. We've talked it over, or rather your mother and I have talked it over. *You* have listened and protested."

Dane grunted, all of a sudden feeling nauseated, like he was going to throw up. He felt lightheaded as he grabbed the doorframe for support.

"Are you *sure* you're okay?" his dad asked.

"I'm going to bed early," he replied, even though sleeping was the farthest thing from his mind.

*Where is Abby?* Dane thought.

"I think you should. I'll come up and check on you later. Would you like me to tuck you in now?"

"Naw, I'm too big for that, Dad," Dane said, managing a fake smile. "You go ahead downstairs. Aunt Betty is waiting."

"Okay," his dad said, and off he went, leaving Dane to clutch the doorjamb and stare at the bird that his family hadn't owned until this very moment.

The bird shifted uneasily on its perch when Dane found his courage and uprooted himself from his spot. Putting his face up to the cage, Dane asked, "Where's Abby?"

"I'm Abby!" the bird shrieked back in its one-tone voice.

"Not you! Where's Abby! The girl!" Dane shouted at it.

"Book!" the bird shot back. "Your Abby gone!"

"Book?"

"Book!" the bird sang again, agitated, shifting from foot to foot on the branch. "What are you, stupid?"

Dane shook his head, trying to clear it. Had he just heard that?

"Go!" the bird squawked at him. "Not too late! Not too late!"

Dane groaned as he ran from the room, slapped off the light, and slammed the door. He ran to his room and shut his own door, but not before he heard Aunt Betty's piercing cackle drifting up from the dining room.

It was a strange reminder that Abby was not around. His Aunt had taken his foster sister's place.

She had disappeared into thin air.

She had ceased to exist.

Thunder rumbled outside as the rain continued to pour.

# CHAPTER FOUR

Dane leaned against the door, breathing heavily, trying to control his feelings and calm down. *Get a grip*, he thought.

What was he going to do now?

His gaze landed on Mr. Hill's *Titanic* book. It was sitting on his desk, the glossy cover reflecting the light of his desk lamp, the painting of the ship slicing through the water hard to see from where he was in the harsh glare.

"He didn't tell me what to do anyway, so why should I do anything?" he mumbled as he walked over and stared at it hatefully. He was too busy. Besides, he had stuff to do. Weekends to plan, video games to play, TV to watch as he drifted off to sleep.

*But not sisters to tease*, he thought. He should have been happy, but he wasn't. He might not want her to live with them, but vanishing into thin air wasn't something that he had in mind either.

Grudgingly he sat down at his desk as he opened the book. He could at least flip through it, he supposed.

It didn't take long for him to become engrossed, and for a while he actually forgot about Abby. Intrigued by the first few pages, Dane flipped more, scanning passages of words and old black and white photographs mixed in with fancy colored drawings and paintings. He marveled, as he often did when faced with books on the *Titanic*, at the many facts and figures.

The *Titanic* struck the iceberg at 11:40 P.M. on a Sunday, after the captain had ignored warnings of an impending ice field. By 2:20 A.M. on Monday morning, she was gone.

It took the ship two hours and forty minutes to go down.

There were over two thousand two hundred people on board the approximately 883-foot ship. Seven hundred of them were survivors, the rest victims.

Close to sixty children had died on board, mostly third-class passengers.

The ship was equipped with only sixteen regular lifeboats and four emergency collapsibles, many of which were launched only partially full. The rest were loaded to overflowing during complete panic and pandemonium. Collapsible A had been half swamped with water and Collapsible B had been launched upside-down.

The ship had a racquetball court, swimming pool and gymnasium.

It had the best third-class accommodations a ship had ever seen.

The ship took one, and only one, voyage.

The facts were amazing to him.

It wasn't until he reached the section of the book that was entitled "Passengers of the *Titanic*" that he found anything out of the ordinary.

Up to that point he had been pouring over the book, fascinated. When he reached the section that displayed old photographs of the passengers, both in candid and non-candid shots, he slowed down his scanning, his eyes wandering over the faces of all the people who didn't have any idea that within a few days they would either be dead or very grateful to still be alive.

Captain Edward Smith.

Charles Lightoller, second officer.

Bruce Ismay, managing director and first-class passenger.

Ida and Isador Strauss, first-class passengers.

Dane's eyes flicked over the faces. Many of them he had seen before in other books, and some he had not.

Margaret Brown, first-class passenger.

Harold Bride and Jack Phillips, wireless operators.

Abby Walsh, third-class passenger.

Dane sucked in his breath.

He brought the book closer to his face; almost close enough to touch his nose. There, on page 165, jammed in next to photographs of officers, crew, and assorted passengers, was his foster sister. It was unmistakable.

She was wearing a dress, and Dane knew her small wardrobe well enough to know that he had never seen that dress before. He couldn't tell what color it was because of the black and white photograph, but nonetheless he was sure. She was also wearing what looked like a small coat over the dress, stockings, and dark leather shoes. A hat with a wide brim complemented her outfit, but it didn't hide the confused look on her face.

It was Abby. No question.

"Some kind of joke?" he mumbled to himself. Some elaborate scheme concocted by the principal and his parents to turn him around, to change the way he felt about her?

Dane mulled it over for a moment thoughtfully. His parents didn't seem like the sort who would do this kind of thing, and Aunt Betty certainly wouldn't be involved. Did the principal have so much time on his hands that he did this with every student who needed a push in what he thought was the right direction? Print up an elaborate, colorful book at a moment's notice?

No way, he thought.

But he had to be sure. He had to be sure his leg wasn't being pulled. He scooped the book off the desk and stood up; deciding he would show it to his parents, and give them a chance to come clean. Just in case. Ha ha, big joke! You know we don't own a bird, here's your sister under the table, now do you appreciate her? Now will you be good to her?

He was on his way to the door, eyes still focused on the photo, when his legs buckled and he staggered weakly backward, almost falling on his bed.

He was in the book, too. He just hadn't noticed before.

Dane had been so shocked to see her in the picture that he hadn't taken the time to search the faces of the people surrounding her.

But there he was.

The photo had obviously been taken just before the first and last voyage of the *Titanic*. It showed what looked like a family, a large family, standing on the poop deck, the dock of Southampton visible behind them. A man and a woman, both of whom looked like they were in their forties, stood with a group of eleven children in front of them. The man stood behind the boys and the woman was standing behind the girls. Abby was among them.

He was, too, looking like he was the oldest there of the boys. He was wearing clothes that looked at home in this book but would get him laughed out of school if he wore them any time soon. It was difficult to tell the color of what he was wearing, but his shorts and jacket looked as if they would be gray or black, and his hat a light brown. His face, like the rest of the faces of the other children, was smile-less, and maybe even a little confused.

For the first time Dane searched for a caption to shed some explanation on this oddity. He found one in small print at the bottom of the page and began to read.

"Mr. and Mrs. George Arthur from London, England, and their group of orphans on their way to New York, riding third-class."

"Oh, wow," he groaned. This just kept getting more and more strange.

Still gripping the book he flopped backward on the bed, feeling lightheaded and not able to believe it all.

He fell into inky blackness.

And slammed onto a bed which was not his own, but a hard bunk which creaked with his weight. He blinked hard as he read the writing on the top bunk above him.

Property of RMS *Titanic*.

# CHAPTER FIVE

"Oh, you've got to be kidding me," Dane said as he rubbed his eyes unbelievingly. He stared again at the stenciled letters above him. They were as solid and black as ever.

"Impossible!" he mumbled, but it was obvious it was true. He supposed he shouldn't have been surprised after all of the weird things that had been happening after the meeting in the principal's office, but all the same, this was bizarre. One moment he was at home, the next moment he was on the *Titanic*. Ridiculous!

Clutched to his chest was the book, still open to the page he had last been studying. A quick glance confirmed that he and Abby were still there, with the same slightly confused expression glued forever in black and white on their faces.

He sat up and whirled his legs off the bunk, narrowly missing knocking his head on the bunk above him. Looking at his legs, he noticed that he was no longer wearing jeans but what looked like striped pajamas. His shoes were gone as well.

*It must be bedtime*, he thought wildly.

For the first time he looked at what was going on about him. Boys a little older than he were bustling about in what looked like a normal bedtime routine. They were carrying around towels and toothbrushes and toiletries kits, some of them looking like they had just gotten out of the shower. The room he was in was lined on all sides by two-level bunk beds. There were some closets, but other than that there was hardly any furniture except for a couple of chairs. The carpet was a deep maroon color and the walls a dark crème.

A boy with a head of bright and wavy red hair, who looked like he was in his late teens, leaned down to Dane's level. As he began to speak he startled Dane.

"What?" Dane asked, feeling stupid and thickheaded and incoherent.

"No reading. Bedtime, right?" the boy said as he reached for Dane's book, which he was still clutching tightly.

"I'll put it away," Dane said quickly.

The boy smiled and lowered his arm. "All right, then," he said as he retreated from Dane's bunk. He spoke in an accent that Dane placed as English, but from what part of England he wasn't sure. He looked like he was the oldest among the boys.

Dane scooted off the bunk and explored under his bed. He saw two sets of duffel bags. He reached for the one under the head of his bunk and pulled the khaki colored bag toward him. The hair stood up on the back of his neck as he turned over the tag and read "DANE SHERIDAN."

Dane noticed the older boy he had been talking to was watching him again, this time suspiciously as he stuffed the book quickly in the bag. "That's not stolen, is it?" he asked. "You're treating it like you don't want me to see it." He approached Dane's bunk and squatted near him.

"No," Dane answered, trying not to sound too defensive. "It's mine."

"Well, let me tell you how I see things," the older boy said, staring hard but not unkindly. "First of all you are an orphan who got caught stealing from other third-class passengers. The master at arms thought about keeping you in the brig until the end of the voyage, but because you didn't seem to be the typical thief, he asked if I would take you in to work for me. I said yes. The way I see it, you owe me."

Dane listened to the lecture with increasing incredulity. He had stolen? When? He had just gotten here!

"What do I owe you?" he finally asked after a lengthy silence while he digested the update of his condition.

"You owe me your honesty," he replied. "I stuck up for you. No one else has or will. You're an orphan on his way from England to America with your foster family to see how many of you can be adopted." The boy smiled at Dane's astonished expression. "I read your file."

"File?" Dane said, the word tumbling thickly out of his mouth.

"Yes. The file I received from your foster father, George Arthur. He is quite a gentleman."

George Arthur must be the man in the picture in the book. The man standing behind the group of boys, Dane figured. At least that's what he recalled from the caption he had only been able to read once.

"Oh," Dane said, trying not to seem too slow or stupid. His mind was reeling from trying to keep up with the turn of events the last five minutes had brought him.

"I know that your parents moved you and your sister to England shortly after she was born," the older boy continued, "and that they died in an accident a couple of years ago. You have been staying with the Arthur's Orphanage, and now they're trying their luck getting all of you adopted in the States." Looking into Dane's eyes he asked, "Is that about right?"

Dane, who could have been told that he had been hatched by a giant chicken on Mars, could only nod in agreement and go with the flow.

Play the game.

"Until then," the older boy added, "you work for me,

understand?"

"Yes," Dane replied. And then, "Doing what?"

"Well, you are a bellboy, which means you do any-thing I ask you to do. Since all of the passengers are already on board and we don't need luggage pushed around, that means delivering messages for passengers. Running the el-evators. That sort of thing."

Inwardly, Dane started to grin. He was going to get to work on the Titanic?

The young man stuck his hand out at Dane. "We weren't properly introduced. I'm Clifford. Everyone on this ship calls me Cliff. Head of bellboys, that's my game."

Dane shook the offered hand solemnly. He didn't know what he had done to get kicked from a third-class passenger to a working bellboy, but he knew this boy had stuck up for him. He knew immediately he was going to like Cliff. Cliff whatever his name was.

"Now, bedtime, right?" Cliff got up from his crouch-ing position and stood to his almost six feet. "Busy day to-morrow with you learning the ropes and all, and you need a rest. And no more stealing," he said as he shook his finger at Dane, trying to look strict. "All right?"

"Okay," Dane assured. And then, as Cliff turned to leave, he asked, "What day is it anyway? I can't remember."

"Friday. Friday the twelfth of April. Does it matter?"

"No," Dane said.

But it did matter. It mattered a lot.

Ten minutes later Dane lay on his back, hands folded behind his head, eyes staring up into the darkness. It was so dark he could hardly make out the words on the bunk above him. The only light that crept in was the little that made its way underneath the door from the constantly lit hall. The bunks holding his sleeping workmates around the room were just dim shapes to him, hardly visible.

The ship was quiet, except for some footsteps occasionally in the hall and the soft, rhythmic, soothing hum of the engines. He marveled that there was barely any ship movement. He had once seen a movie on the *Titanic* that had been filmed with the camera gently rocking back and forth, trying to simulate a ship at sea, which he thought at the time had been silly. He had read accounts of Titanic passengers who had said most of the time they had been able to forget that they were even on a ship.

He found this to be true. If he hadn't known for a fact that he was on the *Titanic*, he might not have known he was on a ship at all. It was smooth sailing.

Staring into the dark he reflected that just a short time ago he had been eating dinner with his parents. And now here he was in another place, another time, far from home. And somewhere was his foster sister, Abby. He wondered for the first time how she was taking all of this. He hadn't actually been alive in 1912 when the photograph in the book was taken, and neither had she, but their faces in the photograph relayed how both of them felt right now.

Confused.

Confused, and, at least for him, a little excited.

He listened to the sound of the other boys as they slept. The slow, cadenced breathing, and the occasional snores gave them away. He had noticed it hadn't taken them long to drift off and figured Cliff probably worked them hard all day long, doing whatever it was that bellboys did.

Dane thought he could hear Cliff's deeper snoring on a bottom bunk in the corner of the room. He was surprised that no one stood guard or watched the boys at night. He must be in a group of people who held trusted positions and were responsible workers and didn't need a babysitter.

But could *he* be trusted? Evidently not. He had stolen something. He guessed it didn't matter what it had been or to whom it had belonged. His punishment was obviously working as a bellboy or staying in the ship's version of jail.

He was sure he preferred this.

He wondered how long it would take him to get used to his situation and fit in with the others. Today was Friday, almost Saturday. He knew the ship struck the iceberg on Sunday evening. He would have to get used to his surroundings quickly if he wanted to...

To what?

To save his foster sister from the fate to which the *Ti-*

*tanic* was destined. All of this was happening because of Mr. Hill, wasn't it? After all, Mr. Hill had given him the book. The principal knew that this was going to happen. Looking at it now, Dane grudgingly thought to himself that it was an unfair punishment. He had been mean, rude and uncaring to his sister, but landing on the *Titanic*, a doomed ship?

Dane's eyelids were getting heavy and his mind was becoming weary from tossing his situation around. He pulled back the left sleeve of his pajamas and hit the light on his watch.

His watch!

Dane's grin was lit by the bright glow of his out-of-place timepiece. He quickly slipped under the blanket. His clothes hadn't made the trip to the *Titanic*, but his watch had. It was as if a friend had been allowed to come along with him on the trip. With this he would be able to keep a close eye on the time as it counted down to disaster and not become confused and have to ask every other passenger what time it was.

Dane looked at the date and grinned again when he saw it said zero four slash twelve slash twelve. April 12, 1912. His watch even knew the correct date.

It was ten o'clock. This was about the time his parents liked him to go to bed on school nights, although he often tried to push it to ten fifteen if he could. Back in Silver Rush it was Thursday, soon to be Friday. He chuckled when he thought of school.

Guess he wouldn't be going.

Would he be missed? Marked absent?

Would his parents miss him at home, or would he cease to exist, like Abby? Would regular time pass, or would he make it home in the blink of an eye?

Would he make it home? Was he forever stuck in time? This was a game without a clear objective. It was a game that you played and hopefully learned the rules as you went along. He was on his own.

And what of Abby? What if he couldn't save her?

He shuddered at the thought. It was one thing to not like her that much, but another to let her die. Would she really perish with all the rest of the *Titanic's* doomed passengers?

Dane shook his head. You could go nuts thinking about this.

Sticking his head out from under the blanket he twisted onto his stomach and quietly pulled his duffel bag out from under the bunk. His fingers fumbled in the darkness for the book. Finding it, he rolled over onto his back and flipped it open. *Too dark to see much*, he thought. Dane slipped under the blanket again. He took off his watch, and held it close to the book, his thumb hitting the light button. After a moment he found the page with Abby and himself on it and took one more long, lingering look.

Finally, reluctantly, he let go of the light button; afraid he would burn it out the one time in his life he needed it the most. Ready to get some badly needed sleep he shut the book, and as he did, something fell out of the back. Dane held it up to his watch as he turned on the light.

It was Abby's waxed leaf art project.

Dane studied the front of it for a moment before he flipped it over to investigate the back. The dim light illuminated the words Abby Walsh, and then below that the words: To my big brother Dane.

Dane felt tears sting his eyes and he wiped them furiously with the back of his hand.

How had this gotten here? Was it another of the principal's little tricks? He slipped the book back in the duffel and shoved it back underneath the bunk.

Lying down on his thin pillow he slipped Abby's artwork underneath it and closed his eyes.

# CHAPTER SIX

It seemed like absolutely no time had passed in between the time Dane had closed his eyes last night and now. He was abruptly awakened by the sound of Cliff's voice thundering through the small room, complete with its crisp English accent.

"Come on, lads! Rise and shine! Errands to run and tips to earn! Let's go! Anyone of you may become rich today!"

Dane heard several of the boys groan, and he promptly joined in with them. "What time is it?" he heard one of them ask.

"Time to get going!" was the cheerful reply.

Dane turned his head in time to see Cliff snap on the lights to a chorus of more groans. The young man was resplendent in his head bellboy uniform, which, Dane assumed, was just a bigger version of the one he would be wearing. As if his mind were being read, Cliff went to an open closet and retrieved a maroon bellboy uniform on a hanger, which he brought to Dane.

"You can wear this one," Cliff said brightly. "It belonged to the boy who quit when we got to Ireland. Took a shore leave and never returned. I've been short-handed ever since."

Dane roused himself from his bunk as Cliff held the uniform at shoulder height on him. "Yeah. Sure. That's about right," he muttered. "So it's a little long. You can roll up the pants some. It'll do."

Dane took the uniform and, noting than none of the other boys seemed overly shy, changed quickly and pushed his folded pajamas in his duffel bag, on top of the *Titanic* book. Then he buckled the straps to the bag.

"Get up, Master Watson! Time's a wastin'!" Dane heard Cliff say as he turned just in time to see the chief bellboy grab a boy who looked just a little older than Dane by the legs and pull him rudely on to the carpeted floor. Dane approached him as he brushed some lint off the uniform.

"What do you think?" he asked.

"Roll the legs up," Cliff suggested. "You look fine."

Dane rolled them up, grabbed a toiletries kit from his duffel, and exited the room. He looked to the left and right, searching for the bathroom. He was relieved when Cliff stuck his head out the door and tossed a round bellboy hat to him, and then pointed to the left. As Dane walked the short distance to the door that said Gentleman, he figured that he must have been given into Cliff's care sometime early yesterday evening. Cliff didn't seem a bit surprised that Dane appeared completely clueless as to his whereabouts.

In the bathroom the sight of men and boys of various ages coming and going greeted Dane. Taking showers, brushing teeth, combing hair, it was all being done. Dane stood in front of a mirror and used water from the sink to flatten his hair with his fingers. He put on the hat and straightened the thick costume he was wearing, and then took a step back to take a look at himself.

The uniform was a deep maroon color. A single row of eight buttons ran from the neck to the waist, and gold braiding adorned the end of each sleeve. The gold braiding also decorated the sides of his pant legs and ran from his waist down to the black shoes on his feet. A maroon pillbox hat with a chinstrap, also embroidered in gold braiding, topped off his uniform.

He *did* look good.

He finished his bathroom duties and found his way back to the bellboy room, which was conveniently labeled BELLBOYS in bold letters. Before he could open it the door sprang open and Cliff came out in front of the other boys.

"Breakfast," Cliff said to him jovially, and out went the line of boys. Cliff stepped back and counted them all as they lined up against the wall in the hall and waited.

Dane counted too, silently. Ten. And he and Cliff made twelve. Dane fell into line at the back after he had tossed his bathroom kit on his bunk as Cliff rejoined the front. He noticed his stomach growling and felt a wave of hunger hit him as he realized it had been a long time since his last meal of spaghetti with Aunt Betty. It seemed like ages ago.

It had been ages ago. Ages in the future.

He was jolted from his thoughts by the boy ahead of him who was saying something to him.

"What?" Dane questioned.

"Thief," the boy repeated.

Dane stared incredulously at the older boy, who looked like he was about fourteen. He was a little taller than Dane and stockier, almost on the verge of being fat. He was wearing round glasses, which he pushed up on his nose as he walked more briskly under Dane's stare. What blonde hair Dane observed on the boy was cut short.

"I'm not a thief," Dane replied defiantly. "I was framed."

"Sure," said the boy. His accent, like Cliff's, was also English.

"What's your name?" Dane questioned.

"Roger," he replied. Disinterested now in Dane, he turned and walked, eyes frontward, in a rather quick and prissy way that made Dane smile with amusement. Nice to see he had made a friend on his first day on the job.

As Dane walked down the corridor following Cliff (he felt only slightly like a baby duckling being led by its mother) he caught sight of a sign that said E Deck. At least now he knew what level he was on.

As Cliff led them up sets of stairs and through the maze of the ship it occurred to Dane how hard this was going to be. His mission had become obvious, the object of the game clear. He was here to save his sister. Foster sister. That's how he would win the game. He didn't know if this was really a game, a dream, or an illusion, but it sure felt real, and he was pretty sure he wasn't dreaming. If this were a dream he would be able to kick back and wait for his mom to shake him awake for school. But when he woke up this morning there had been no sign of Mom or Dad, room or TV.

He wasn't sure how he was going to do it, but he was going to get to Abby. He was going to find her on this whale of a ship and stop it from sinking—if he could. It would be a tough job, but somehow he would do it. He would save the *Titanic* in this game. He was pretty sure it was just a game, but he would play along. It might even be fun. He would make it fun.

And what if it wasn't a game?

He had to take it seriously.

Passing down a corridor on C Deck, Cliff halted his group of boys outside a door that said Crew Galley. They entered and Dane found himself in a room filled with men and women of all ages. Some were clean, some dirty. Some were in uniform; some were in filthy undershirts that had once probably been white. Some had braces clinging to dirty pants that hung over even dirtier boots. Some of the women wore clean dresses with white lace. This was obviously the room where maids, firemen, mechanics, and assorted other crew members came to eat. Dane guessed some of them were here for breakfast like he was, and some were the evening crew getting off of their shifts and were about to turn their breakfast into dinner before going to bed. The hustle and bustle of the bare, plain white room filled with tables and noise was astonishing.

Dane and the rest of the boys stood in a long line to get their bread and oatmeal, which he then carried to a table with the others and began to eat ravenously.

It was partway through his breakfast that Dane snuck a peak at his digital watch and saw the time. It was 7:30 A.M. on Saturday, April thirteenth.

Was that enough time to save Abby? Not really. He figured that after breakfast he would be herded off by Cliff and made to do God only knew what. How much time would that eat up? If he were going to make this work, he would have to be sneaky, clever, and come up with a plan.

All of the boys around him seemed to know each other and were chatting up a storm. Dane probably wouldn't be missed if he were to leave. Standing, he left the rest of his breakfast and slipped out of the room the same way he had come.

He had to find Abby, and soon.

He retraced his steps and before long had entered the bellboy room and shut the door. After a few fumbles at the switch (you didn't flip a switch, you punched a button, he discovered) the room lit up. White light from the bulb as well as sunlight through the round windows streamed in on Dane as he dug the book out of his duffel and sat on the edge of the bunk. He would start with this and move on from here. He hadn't yet been able to research it nearly as much as he wanted and needed to.

Dane flipped the book open to the photograph that held the image of Abby and himself. The caption read: George and Lillian Arthur, the owners and operators of Arthur's Orphanage in London, England. They are shown with a number of their young charges, almost all of who had homes waiting for them in America. Third-class passengers were divided according to male and female on the ship. Mr. Arthur stayed with the boys in the bow section of the ship and Mrs. Arthur accompanied the girls in the stern.

None of these passengers survived.

Dane gasped audibly when he reached the final line of the caption.

"None survived?" he mouthed. He knew that the losses in third-class were staggering, that many of the steerage passengers had been trapped below decks behind locked gates. But to lose entire families? It was almost incomprehensible.

Roger sticking his head into the room, looking completely ridiculous in his round hat, interrupted him. "Cliff wants you back in the dining room," Roger said in a smugly superior way. He added, "Right now!"

"Okay, okay," Dane grumbled as he stood. He shielded the book away from Roger with his body, waiting for Roger to leave before he packed it away again.

But he didn't leave. He remained where he was, his head still poking from the door like a turtle peaking from a shell. "What have you got?"

"Nothing," Dane said as he bent and packed it back into the duffel bag and buckled the straps.

"Uh huh," Roger said, unconvinced. He eyed the bag suspiciously as Dane approached the door and shut off the lights. Together, the two boys went back to the dining hall.

To say Cliff was displeased would have been like saying the *Titanic* was big. Dane read his face and knew he was about to get ripped up by his new boss.

"Where have you been?" Cliff growled, standing from his bench as Dane and Roger approached.

"I had to—" Dane began. It was just as well he didn't finish. He hadn't known what he was going to say anyway.

"You are not allowed to leave my side unless I tell you to," Cliff began. "The only reason you're not in the brig is because I stood up for you. If you go off again and get into trouble, both you and I will get it from the master at arms, or maybe even the captain. And I can't afford to lose my job."

Both Dane's and Cliff's faces were turning red from shame or anger. He didn't want to let Cliff in on what was going on, at least not yet. How could he tell Cliff he wasn't doing anything wrong?

Cliff tore his scrutinizing gaze from Dane and glared at Roger, who had been standing next to Dane now looking smugly amused. "Don't you have something better you could be doing?"

Roger looked hurt. "Not really—"

"Sit down!" Cliff commanded.

Roger left sullenly and moped his way back to his seat out of earshot of Dane and Cliff.

"That's Roger," said Cliff, using a more casual tone. His expression had lightened some. "He's always into everyone's business. That means that someday he'll probably make captain, right?"

Dane smiled faintly but was beginning to feel a sense of doom mixed with urgency. If he wasn't allowed to stray from Cliff, how was he going to get his sister, or even see her? And, for that matter, if he did get her, what was he supposed to do with her? The *Titanic* probably wasn't equipped with a helicopter.

Cliff turned serious again as he peered into Dane's eyes. "Can I trust you?"

"What?" Dane asked. He had been wistfully thinking about air rescues.

"Can I trust you?"

Dane weighed the question, and then nodded. "You can trust me," he replied finally. What he really wanted to do was run off and search the ship, but he knew he would get caught and tossed in jail. That wouldn't do *anyone* any good.

"That's good," Cliff said. "Because the jobs that you will be doing for me require a man who is trustworthy. I don't even know why I took you on if you did steal, because you will be entrusted with all kinds of tasks. If you're a thief, then you're the wrong man for this job."

"Entrusted with what?" Dane questioned. He didn't know, he realized, what his job was. Something about delivering messages. Is that what Cliff had said last night?

"You're running errands for me and delivering telegrams, mostly in first-class, but all over the ship, if needed.

I'm being paid to supervise the bellboys and liftboys, and I
need only the best men to help me out."

"Liftboys?"

"They run the elevators."

Oh. *Lift*boys. Dane shook his head. He should have
known. Gosh, he felt stupid.

# CHAPTER SEVEN

A half an hour later life had completely changed for the better for Dane.

So this was what a bellboy did.

Attached to his belt was a set of keys that, if attached to the strongest man in the world, would still make him list slightly to one side. The ring had almost every key imaginable on it including gate keys to the different class divisions. There were room keys, kitchen cabinet keys, storage room keys, you name it, and he had been entrusted with them. He could see why Cliff was so anxious about how his bellboys looked and acted.

*It certainly wouldn't do to have a thief carrying a bunch of keys like this around,* he thought.

The keys banged together and jingled as he walked the halls of the ship. Not just any halls, but the halls of the first-class section. Since the classes were at times strewn all about the ship, he had been asked to deliver a message from one first class passenger to another. A first-class passenger near the bow on B Deck wanted to communicate with a passenger on C Deck via Cliff and now via Dane. Off he was, an entrusted employee on the White Star Line's *Titanic*, on an errand.

What other boy in the world, his own world, could brag of that?

As he went his smile was infectious. He waved and grinned at everyone he saw, whether they were crewmembers or passengers of any class, and most of them returned his smile or wave. He couldn't think of much that could destroy his good mood.

Along with the keys clanking noisily on his belt he had folded in his pocket a miniature blueprint of the *Titanic*. Cliff had explained that bellboys had to know the layout of the ship, and since none of them had been able to have much of a tour, they had all been given maps. Dane had been wondering how anyone could find his or her way around the huge ship. Cliff had told Dane that the bellboys had only had a few hours training before the voyage. Cliff had also warned Dane that sometimes passengers called the bellboys "buttons" (due to the amount of buttons on their uniform), so he should be aware what that term meant. It amused Dane that he was to be classified by an accessory on his uniform. He was glad he wouldn't be called "pillbox", after his hat.

Some of the problems Dane had been tossing about in his mind were on the road to being solved. He had been concerned about how he was going to have access to the ship to see Abby. Problem solved with the keys. He had also wondered about how he was going to know where to go to see his foster sister. Problem solved with the maps in his pocket. The third problem involved when he was going to see her, and that problem had been solved a few minutes ago with the rest of Dane's dilemmas.

"I only have eleven of you, so we'll be working hard from now until eight o'clock with only breaks for lunch and dinner," Cliff had explained after he had turned over the map and keys to Dane. "And I really only have seven of you, since four others are working the lifts, so you will be working nonstop. But you will get an hour break for lunch, all right?"

"Great!" Dane had replied enthusiastically.

Third problem solved.

Cliff's "office," if that was what you wanted to call it, was located in a corner of the sumptuous first-class lounge (modeled after the Palace of Versailles in France) just off of the Boat Deck. The bellboys were to report there to get each new assignment. Dane would go back and forth from Cliff's office to various parts of the ship until lunchtime, and then he would be off for an hour. From one until six he would do more work in this manner. From six to seven was dinner, and then he had to rush back to meet Cliff by seven. From seven until eight he would do a few more runs, and then have free time until bedtime.

Exhausting.

Dane stopped and pulled the papers from his pocket. He was hopelessly lost. Cliff had told all of them to use their maps if they got confused or turned around, and here he was with a message for a Mr. John Morris in room C94 and he was at the entrance to the second-class library.

Oops. He groaned and hunted again.

At last he located C94 and knocked on the door. The man who opened it looked rich and impatient. He took the message from Dane with not even so much as a thank you and handed Dane what looked like a dime.

"It's a sixpence," the man said as Dane stared at the coin, trying to figure out what it was. "You must be a Yank."

"Yes," Dane replied, but the impatient man had already shut the door. Guessing this treatment was normal, he pocketed the coin and headed back to A Deck to see what Cliff had for him to do next.

When eleven-thirty rolled around Dane thought it couldn't have come any sooner. He had worked his legs off running through all parts of the ship delivering all sorts of messages, gifts and telegrams. He was starving and looking forward to lunch like he had never looked forward to a meal before in his life.

Most of the messages that Cliff gave him to deliver were written down and he had no problem delivering those. The going rate for his tip seemed to be about a nickel if the passenger was an American, and a sixpence if the passenger was English, although on a couple of occasions he had been stiffed and hadn't received anything at all.

The most entertaining one he had come across so far was when he had been requested to sing "Happy Birthday" to a first-class female passenger. Dane had been the third boy Cliff had asked to do it and he had accepted grudgingly, not being a true believer in his voice, afraid he would hit the wrong notes and make a fool of himself. He wasn't the best singer in church or school, but he had at last decided to give it a shot, at least partially to remain on Cliff's good side.

And besides, who could refuse a guaranteed tip of a shilling?

He had done okay, had only turned a little pink in the face, and had graciously accepted a whole pound when the birthday woman had screamed with delight and hugged and kissed him, making her fiancé all the more pleased with his performance.

Dane had let himself be hugged and smiled sheepishly at the woman's assessment of his song.

He had smelled alcohol.

He had spent the morning bustling down endless corridors, maps in his hand, keys on his belt, and a brainful of names and numbers he had to keep straight. Most of his work was for the first-class passengers who didn't feel like traveling from one floor to another, or who enjoyed the novelty of having someone on board a ship run around and deliver messages. Sometimes he was asked to deliver from the crew to passengers or from passengers to the crew, but he never delivered from second or third-class, only to them.

They didn't have access to the first-class lounge and Cliff's message service.

"Have you been up on deck much?" Cliff asked Dane after he had finished running a message from one first-class passenger to another confirming a squash game. Dane, who had done not so much as glance out a window, shook his head.

"No sir, I haven't," Dane replied.

Cliff smiled. "I appreciate the sir, but it's not needed from you. I don't usually get that from anyone around here. Seems my uniform tells most of the passengers around here I'm someone who can be stepped on." He jerked his thumb in the direction of the first-class passengers who were milling about in the lounge and rolled his eyes. "Oh well," he continued. "Guess I won't be a senior bellboy forever, in charge of all you little runts now, will I?"

*No*, Dane thought miserably, *you probably wouldn't*. It occurred to him for the first time that many of these people wandering cheerfully about were going to be dead by tomorrow night if he wasn't able to do anything. He choked back the thought.

"Ready for lunch? Come on, let's go," Cliff said enthusiastically. "We'll bring it out on deck."

"Are we allowed to do that?" Dane asked, eyebrows raised.

"No," Cliff responded.

Twenty minutes later Dane and Cliff sat in Lifeboat Number Nine on the second-class Promenade Deck, jamming sandwiches in their mouths. They had thrown back the canvas cover and were enjoying the stiff April breeze as it blew over them in their gently rocking boat; they were oblivious to the strange looks they received now and then. They had brought the sandwiches up from the galley after Cliff had given the other bellboys strict instructions to meet him in his office at one o'clock to attend to a new set of duties. The lift operators had hung signs announcing, Lifts Closed, Use Stairs, in front of their elevators and had left in search of food.

Dane snuck a look at his watch when Cliff had his head turned the other way. 11:55 A.M. It would have been later if Cliff hadn't let them go a little early. Time was ticking and he needed to be on the move soon, but this thought didn't make him enjoy his lunch in the lifeboat any less.

It was a bright, crisp day. The cool breeze was ruffling Dane's hair, hair that was not cut quite as short as many other crewmembers. Dane had noticed this but had been fearful the ship's barber would soon be chasing him about with a pair of shears if he pointed it out.

His hat sat on the bench beside him as he munched contentedly, watching smoke pour from the first three smoke stacks. He wondered for just a moment if anyone famous would be sitting in this lifeboat tomorrow night. He supposed he could always look it up later, although if he had his way history would be rewritten by tomorrow night anyway.

"This is great," Dane mentioned to Cliff at last after a long, happy silence, and then almost wished that he hadn't said anything. He had very much enjoyed the way he had been listening to virtually nothing other than the sound of the wind winding its way around the smokestacks.

"Isn't it?" Cliff replied. "We're not really supposed to be here, but at least we're not in the first-class section. The second-classers don't seem to mind quite as much. Not enough to report us, anyway."

Dane crumpled up the wax paper his food had come in and crammed it in his empty pocket just in time to see Cliff toss his garbage overboard. He was tempted to mention it, but then held off when he thought of a more important issue that was nagging at him.

Tentatively, he said, "Hey, I know someone in third-class I would like to see—"

"Your sister?" Cliff asked, chewing.

"Yeah. How did you know?"

"Captain of the bellboys, remember? I know everything!" Cliff smiled at Dane, but Dane could tell by his expression he wasn't really kidding.

"I make it my business to know as much as I can, and I knew you were traveling with her," Cliff continued. "I figured sooner or later you would want to visit her."

"I do," Dane replied eagerly. "But I wasn't sure where to start looking-"

Dane suddenly stopped himself, realizing he was about to talk himself into a trap. He had been about to tell Cliff he didn't know where she was staying, and how would that look? It would almost be admitting that he hadn't been on the ship the whole time.

Cliff, however, didn't seem to notice. He handed Dane a piece of paper. "I figured since the men in third-class are in one section of the ship and the women in another, you might not have seen exactly where she was staying, so I found out for you."

Dane breathed a subtle sigh of relief as he opened the folded scrap of paper. It said: Abby Walsh, Room 221, G Deck.

"Thanks!" Dane almost shouted. "I—"

A sudden rocking of the lifeboat made him halt in mid-sentence. Both he and Cliff pitched forward, Dane throwing out his hands to catch himself. He caught sight of Roger's bespectacled face leering at him over the edge of the boat.

"Whatcha' doin'?" Roger asked.

Trying to avoid you, Dane would have liked to have said, but answered simply, "Having lunch. We just finished, actually."

"Oh," Roger said. He let go of the boat and it pitched again, rocking Dane back as he tried to keep his head from greeting the side of the boat.

Cliff and Dane observed Roger walking up the deck toward the bow, looking left and right, then left and right, as if he were standing at a busy traffic light. Dane thought he resembled a sprinkler.

"He looks like he's searching for something to get into, doesn't he?" Cliff commented.

Dane swung himself out of the boat. Lunch had been enjoyable in the "bigger-than-they-looked in photographs" lifeboat. He thought briefly how strange it was that at least one of the boats had been loaded with less than fifteen people. It gave him a case of the willies knowing he had been sitting in a boat that would be the difference between life and death for some people tomorrow night if history didn't change.

"Yeah, he's something else," Dane answered. "Kind of nosey, isn't he?"

"Yes. He's the perfect bellboy," Cliff commented. "He knows where everything is, where everyone is, and the layout of the ship. I wouldn't have chosen him, though. I don't like the way he seems to want to know everyone's business."

"Why did you hire him?" Dane asked as he watched the retreating figure. He couldn't put an exact finger on it, but Roger was beginning to annoy him.

"I didn't hire him," Cliff answered in a mockingly defensive voice. "I don't know who did. Someone at the White Star Line office, I suppose. I was just told he would be one of my bellboys. I didn't get to hire anyone."

"Except me," Dane said with a grin.

Cliff grinned back. "Yes, except you."

# CHAPTER EIGHT

It was now 12:15 P.M. He had forty-five minutes to find his sister, talk to her, and get back to Cliff. He walked briskly down the halls, keys still jingling up a storm on his belt, maps growing sweaty in his hot hands. If someone from the present were watching, they would have thought he was training for the fast walk category in the Olympics, minus perhaps the flying elbows.

Dane went downstairs, around corners, and let himself through numerous gates. It would be his luck that his sister was in the very back of the ship on the last floor that held passengers.

He wiped the sweat from his face with his sleeve. He was cooking in this uniform. Outside it was one thing in the crisp April air. Inside the ship, though, it could be pure torture. If he had any weight to lose, this would be the way to go.

At last he reached his sister's room and breathed a sigh of relief. He knocked on the door and shifted his weight from foot to foot excitedly, looking very much like he was in need of the facilities. It wasn't long before a stern looking face peered out of the door, an expression of curiosity on her features.

Dane recognized her immediately as Mrs. Arthur from the photograph.

The sternly curious expression she was wearing melted when she saw who it was. She flung the door open wide, making it bang and causing Dane to jump. He had thought he would have been in trouble, for stealing whatever it was he had taken.

But her reaction was the exact opposite of what he had prepared himself for. Instead, she threw her arms around him and gave him a bone-crushing hug.

"I was so worried about you," she said in her thick English accent. It was something he would have to get used to, being that he had never been abroad in his ten years. He had never been around so many English people in his life.

"I'm okay," he said to her when she had released him a bit. "I'm working as a bellboy now."

"Do you think I don't know that?" she admonished, but Dane could hear real pride in her voice. "From thief to bellboy. Who would have thought? If it hadn't been for that Clifford, who knows where you would be now."

"I'd like to see—" he began, but the woman he guessed was basically his mother swept him inside the room.

"Of course you want to see your sister, dear," she said briskly. Then she bellowed, "Boy in the cabin, girls!"

Dane winced as the room was filled with panicked screams as the girls scrambled for cover. Dane saw Abby jump down off a top bunk and dodge various toys and books to get to him, her face alight with surprise and excitement.

"Dane!" she cried as she flung herself at him. "How did you get here?"

"How did *you* get here?" Dane answered, returning the same bone-crushing hug he had received from Mrs. Arthur. It was amazing to him how things could change from day to day. Sometimes the things you had you didn't want, and sometimes the things you couldn't have you would fight for. Yesterday he had been all but pushing her away, and today he was trying to make her brains leak out her ears.

"I'm going to take my sister out in the hall and visit, okay?" he asked Mrs. Arthur.

"Of course," she replied as she shooed the two of them out the door. "Bring her back soon!" she called after them.

There was a staircase that led upward near the door, and Dane led Abby by the hand. They had a seat on the third stair up.

"I don't have much time," Dane said as he looked at his watch. Having it made him feel a bit like cheating, like having aces up his sleeves in a poker game, but somehow it had come with him. He wasn't about to argue.

She looked crestfallen. "You can't stay?"

"No, and even if I could I would have to be in the front of the ship with Mr. Arthur and the other boys."

She continued to look sad, but nodded.

"Do you know where we are?" Dane asked.

Her eyes widened. "We're on the *Titanic*," she answered in an awed whisper, leaning close to him. "Do you know about the *Titanic*? It sinks!"

"I know it does," Dane replied. Her face mirrored the way he felt inside, in the pit of his stomach.

"The RMS *Titanic*!" Abby added. "Royal Male Steamer. Does that mean the ship is a boy?"

Dane grinned. "I think its mail, like the kind you send."

"Oh," she said, nodding. Then she asked, "How did we get here?" She fumbled with the hem of her dress nervously, pulling at some loose threads. Dane noticed the dress she was wearing was the same one she had been wearing in the photograph, only now it was a deep shade of green. He thought how interesting it was that when he looked at a black and white photograph he always made the assumption that the black and brown and white clothes were just that–black and brown and white.

How foolish. Of course they had colors back then.

Back now.

"I think this whole thing is my fault," he confessed at last to her. "I can't go into it much now, but we've been sent here to teach me a lesson, I suppose."

Abby looked blankly at him, not understanding. "I was walking home from school and all of a sudden I was walking on this ship in these funny clothes!" Her eyes widened even more on her small face, as big as saucers. "I asked someone where I was, and she looked at me funny. She said I was on the *Titanic!*"

"We are," Dane said resignedly, recognizing this as a fact he couldn't alter. They were going to have to see this adventure through to its end. No bumps on the head from a rough playground game that he could awake from and say, "Whew, I'm glad that's over."

"This ship sinks!" Abby repeated in her harsh whisper. "Do you know when?"

Dane wrestled for a moment with whether or not he should tell her, then said finally, "Tomorrow. It hits the iceberg at 11:40 P.M."

Abby gasped. "Tomorrow? What are we going to do?" Her eyes, still huge, began to fill up with tears.

Dane, a bit alarmed, put his arm around her and pulled her close. It felt awkward at first, but as she put her head on his shoulder and sobbed with frustration at their situation and relief that he was there for her, it began to feel natural. Like he really was her brother.

"Don't cry," he said, trying to sound sure of himself, which, of course, he really wasn't. Inside he felt the same way she did. He had been so busy lately trying to keep up with who he had become, the layout of the ship, his job, and all of the new people around him that he had had very little time to work out much of a plan.

It was time to formulate a plan, and to be specific. Not just, "I'm going to save the ship..."

"I think I'll talk to the captain," Dane said at last as his mind whirled to find answers he didn't yet have for her unanswered question. "I'll go straight to the captain tomorrow and tell him what is going to happen. If that doesn't work, I'll come and get you." Then he added, "I'll come anyway before 11:40 P.M. and tell you what happened."

"Aren't you way on another side of the ship?" Abby asked as her hands continued to worry the hem of her dress to death.

"Yeah, but I've got keys," he said importantly, jiggling them triumphantly for her to see on his belt.

"But what happens if I'm not here?"

"Where else would you be? You'll all be in bed."

"But what if you come too late and we're gone?"

"If I can't get to the captain or I can't change his mind

and I think we're going to hit, I'll let you know as quick as I can."

Abby still looked worried. "But what if you're really late and we're not in our room? How will you be able to find us?"

Dane smiled. "You guys will be easy to find."

"We will?" Abby questioned, unconvinced.

"Oh, yeah. I'll find you by the trail of dolls you guys will leave in the hall."

Abby surprised Dane by grinning from ear to ear, and then she broke into delighted laughter. She gave him a friendly wallop on the arm in an affectionate sisterly manner. Dane was faintly aware that he didn't even mind. He might be able to deal with this sibling thing after all, if they were able to get off of this ship.

Abby's smile faded and she looked shyly at Dane. She shifted her weight uncomfortably as she asked, "Did you steal? Mrs. Arthur said you stole something from one of the passengers and that's why you're not staying with us orphans anymore."

Us orphans. The words rang out in Dane's head. Poetic justice at its finest, it seemed. One day Dane was ragging on his orphaned foster sister and the next day he was one of them as well. He was without a home, and up for adoption in this lesson or game or whatever it was.

The tables had turned.

Life was cruel.

Dane finally shrugged helplessly. "I guess I did but I don't even know what I stole. I just got here, like you." Dane stopped, struggling to find the words that would help Abby understand. "Have you ever walked into a movie halfway through? In the middle?"

Abby brightened. "One time I did. I didn't understand much after that."

"Exactly," Dane sighed, relieved. "You and I came into this in the middle. I'm not positive what we did or who we are supposed to be. I don't even think it matters what I stole or whom I stole it from. We just kind of were...were dropped into the middle of this whole thing."

"So whoever you were stole, but not you?" Abby asked.

Dane smiled. "Yeah, that's it. I may have some problems, but I wouldn't steal like my boss said I did."

"Your boss? Your bellman boss?"

"Yeah. My bellman boss," Dane said with amusement in his voice. "They were going to throw me in the ship's jail, but Cliff said he would take me on to work for him."

"Is it fun?"

Actually, it is. Better than being in the brig."

"Brig?"

"Jail."

"Oh."

Dane looked at his watch, so out of place in the elegant surroundings of the *Titanic*. It even looked out of place in steerage.

He stood. "It's 12:40 P.M. I've gotta go. It's going to take me awhile to get back up to first-class." He tried to ignore the crestfallen look on Abby's face, but he couldn't help but feel sorry for her, trapped on this huge ship with a bunch of people she had been tossed in with. At least he could move around.

"Do you have to go?" she implored. "Can't you stay just for a little while longer?"

"Better not. But remember, I'll be back to get you tomorrow night."

Abby's face lightened a little. "Okay," she said as she threw her small arms around him again. He hugged her back, promising himself as she did he would do everything in his power to get them out of here. The thought that continued to haunt him bounded into his head again: *What if this isn't a game? Could they really die?*

He wasn't willing to sit on his haunches and wait for the ship to go down to find out.

"Promise?" she asked.

"Promise," he said. He walked her back to the door and was about to rap on it when Abby turned to him.

"How are you going to tell the captain about the ship sinking?" she asked. "I mean, why would he believe you?"

"My secret weapon. My book, *The Life and Death of the Titanic*," Dane replied.

# CHAPTER NINE

Dane wound his way through the immense maze of stairs
and hallways to Cliff and the first-class lounge and more
jobs. There was a bounce to his step that hadn't been there
before. It was 12:50 P.M., he was on time, he had seen Abby,
and everything was going his way.

And the book. He had the book. How could he not
save the ship from sinking when he had access to the three
hundred page cheat sheet the principal had given him?

All he had to do was find the captain and show it to
him, and boom, there it was. No sunken ship in the North
Atlantic. It was a failsafe plan. Once the captain saw the
book, he would slow the ship down. Perhaps he would find
some binoculars for the men in the crow's nest to spot the
iceberg. Then Dane remembered reading that they didn't
have any and had left them behind. Maybe the captain
would stop the ship altogether until morning. Something.

He entered the first-class lounge at 12:57 P.M., ready to get another batch of assignments from Cliff. Out of his peripheral vision he spotted Roger in the corner by a table, eyeballing a group of men who were playing cards.

Dane halted his stride, sensing something was amiss. Roger should be delivering whatever Cliff had given him that he was holding in his hands.

Nonchalantly Dane moved into an unoccupied corner of the room, tucking himself away behind a potted plant on a stand to have a gander. He looked left and right to see if anyone was questioning his appearance like he was questioning Roger's.

No one seemed to have seen him.

As he watched, the small group of men stood. One of them who Dane thought he might have seen in the *Titanic* book put his deck of cards into a box and shook hands with the others. They smiled cordially at each other, saying words that Dane couldn't make out, but could only guess.

Something like, "Until this evening, then," or "I'm out for a walk on the deck. Anyone to join me?"

In any event the men left, leaving only a trail of cigarette and cigar smoke behind them.

And something else.

Whatever it was that had caught Dane's eyes had caught Roger's as well. As soon as the men were a safe distance away Roger moved in, appearing to Dane like he was trying to look unhurried, normal. Dane noticed with a quick sweep of his eyes that everyone in the room was paying attention to their own affairs. Drinking, smoking, and talking were the main activities for the men in the room, and they were too wrapped up in what they were doing to notice anyone or anything out of the ordinary.

Roger reached the table and with not so much as a look around him bent down, scooped the object off the floor, and stuffed it into the back of his pants. He pulled the shirt of his uniform over it to cover it up.

It was a wallet.

"Slick," muttered Dane under his breath. "And you called me a thief."

Out went Roger with whatever he had been given by Cliff to deliver, walking as if nothing had happened. Dane stood next to his plant, trying to figure out what to do.

Was this part of the game? What did this have to do with anything?

As much as he wanted to follow Roger, he decided to go see Cliff. He would get into big trouble if he didn't show up soon.

Abandoning his corner he crossed the room and approached Cliff. Cliff smiled and looked at the watch laid out on his desk. "Right on time, Dane," he said approvingly. "Good man. Did you get to see your sister?"

"Yes," Dane replied, feeling angry he wasn't happier

at this moment. He *had* been, until Roger had added this new chapter to his life. Now he had this to deal with. As if a sinking ship wasn't going to be enough. What was he supposed to do now?

Cliff handed a piece of paper to Dane, along with a name and room number. "That's it for now," he said. "Come back when you're done. Take your time. This afternoon is slow."

Dane nodded, deciding he wouldn't tell Cliff what he had seen, at least not yet. What proof did he have? And what would he gain from it anyway? Was it any of his business?

He left Cliff, with job in hand. He exited the lounge, intent on delivering the message, but a tug at his conscience stopped him from heading off in the direction of the Café Parisien on B Deck (he had passed it earlier; he didn't even need his map for it this time). Instead he walked to the edge of the ship and stared over the rail into the cold, blue water. He watched it foam and churn along the side of the ship as he mulled his situation over.

What to do? This game he was playing was much more involved than he had thought earlier. Before, the intent had been to get Abby and get off the ship, if not save it from sinking entirely. What was he to do about this new wrinkle? Did it matter that Roger had seen a dropped wallet during a game of poker and had obviously stolen it?

This was like when you played a board game, intent on heading for the finish, and you kept falling into those various traps laid out for you by those devious game makers.

Go to jail.

Lose a turn.

Go back five spaces.

You have just seen a fellow employee of the White Star Line pilfer a wallet from a first-class passenger. Lose a turn.

Dane sighed. *Better deal with it*, he thought. If not, it would nag at him endlessly.

He turned from the railing and nearly bumped into a passenger who had been standing behind him.

"Excuse me," Dane apologized quickly, waiting for the berating he was sure he would receive from the gentleman who was obviously a member of the first-class elite.

But the man hardly seemed to notice. He was busy patting the front of his tan coat, looking mildly distressed. "No matter," he said absentmindedly. "Say, you haven't by chance seen a wallet, have you?"

Dane looked at the man a little closer. Now he recognized him. It was John Jacob Astor, on his way home from Ireland accompanied by his pregnant wife whose name Dane couldn't recall. Dane had read about him often as one of the better-known personalities that had gone down with the ship.

Before Dane could respond, the man wandered off, his eyes still darting this way and that on the deck.

Was that a hint that he should do something? If so, it was a good one.

Making up his mind to deliver his message given to him by Cliff at the first opportunity, Dane headed to the first place he figured Roger would go, the bellboys' room.

To hide the wallet.

His mind made up, Dane briskly walked through the entrance of the lounge and approached one of his fellow bellboys at the bank of three elevators.

"How 'bout a ride?" He asked.

The bellboy shrugged. "Why not? I'm not busy."

Dane stepped in and the older boy closed the gate and threw the switch. The elevator hummed into life.

"Where to?"

"E Deck, please."

"Your name is Dane?"

Dane nodded. "And yours?"

"Aaron."

They shook hands formally as Dane asked, "Are you gonna be replaced soon?"

Aaron shrugged. "Hope so. Whenever Cliff sends someone else. I don't mind, though. Less running around than doing what you're doing."

"Do you get tips?"

"Sometimes."

Then, casually, Dane probed. "Did Roger come down this way?"

"Yeah. I gave him a ride, too."

The elevator arrived at E Deck and Aaron pulled the switch and opened the gate with a clang. "All aboard who are going to shore," Aaron said with a smile.

"Thanks," Dane said. "Maybe I'll see you later."

"Sure," Aaron replied.

Dane exited and turned the corner and trotted down the long hallway that stretched on for about half the ship. He had heard it referred to as Scotland Road, but wasn't sure why. Was Scotland Road long?

Reaching the door to their room he paused for a moment, wondering what he would say when he confronted Roger. Figuring he would make it up as he went along, he pushed the door open and was greeted by a dark room.

"Roger?" he called, punching the light on.

Nothing. A quick scan around the room and on the bunks revealed that either Roger had come and gone, or else he had never been here.

Dane walked over to Roger's bunk after he had shut the door. Dane knew he wouldn't want anyone going through his own personal things, but this was an exception. Besides, Mr. Astor needed his wallet back.

Dane began to search through Roger's personals. It

wasn't long before he got the brainstorm to lift up Roger's mattress.

There it was.

Dane took the black leather wallet and riffled through it. There was a sizable amount of American currency in it, and Dane guessed that Roger hadn't taken anything. Yet. He tucked the wallet in the back of his pants, pulled the shirt of the uniform over it, and exited the room.

# CHAPTER TEN

Dane was just outside the first-class lounge when Roger bumped into him on his way out, job in hand. If Dane had had time to think about what he should or shouldn't say to Roger, he might have said something more prudent, or perhaps nothing at all.

"Thief," he blurted.

Roger's head swiveled to face Dane. "What?"

"Thief," Dane repeated.

"What are you talking about?"

"I think you know."

Roger's face started to turn red. "Did you see something you'd like to tell me about?"

"What do you think I saw?"

"You tell me."

Dane took a step closer to Roger so that the boys were almost face-to-face. "I think I saw a wallet on the ground under a table, and you pick it up."

Roger's face went a shade redder. "You can't prove anything," he shouted out haughtily.

"Can't I?"

There was silence between the two boys as they stood staring at each other defiantly, eyes locked in mental combat.

Finally Roger spoke. "What can you prove?"

"I've got the wallet you stole from John Jacob Astor," Dane answered. "I'm on my way to return it."

Roger looked genuinely surprised. The surprise mixed together with his anger, making his face contort in a funny way that would have made Dane laugh if the situation hadn't been so intense.

"Then show me! I think you're bluffing! You can't prove anything!" Roger spat out.

"Oh, but I think he can," Cliff said from behind them. The two boys turned to see Cliff and John Jacob Astor standing near them. Cliff smiled slightly, but there was no smile in his eyes to match.

"We heard most of this conversation," he continued. "Dane, do you have something to show us?"

Dane nodded without speaking. He reached behind him and pulled out the wallet from his pants and handed it to Mr. Astor, who took it and thumbed briefly through the currency.

"All here," he said briskly to Cliff. "No harm done."

"How do you know he didn't take it?" Roger asked defensively as he pointed to Dane. "He's the one who has it. Besides, he has a history of this kind of thing and—"

Cliff turned fiercely on Roger as he now stepped nose-to-nose with him. He kept his voice low, but Dane detected a dangerous edge as he spoke.

"First, we overheard the conversation. Second, another passenger saw the whole thing and informed me right before Mr. Astor reported his wallet missing to me." He turned to John Astor. "Sir, it is my duty to inform you that you may press charges if you would like."

The elegant yet realistic man shook his head. "Oh, I don't think that will be necessary. I don't want to create any trouble. But I would like to reward the young man who found it and was on his way to turn it in." He pulled a twenty from his newly found wallet and handed it to Cliff. "With your permission, sir."

Cliff nodded and handed the bill to Dane, who quickly refused it. "No, thank you, sir," he said.

John Astor smiled, Cliff beamed with pride, and Roger added a scowl to his reddened face.

"But I insist," the man said. "All good deeds must be rewarded."

Dane reluctantly took the bill from Cliff.

"Well, I declare this matter over," Mr. Astor said.

"Gentleman, I wish you a good day. I'm off to see Kitty."

"Your wife?" Dane asked.

"My dog," Colonel Astor replied with a smile. And with that he strolled off in the direction of the stern.

Cliff spun on Roger a second time, his face set and angry. "And what am I supposed to do with you now? Am I supposed to keep you on too, despite this? Am I a haven for juvenile thieves?"

"I didn't—" Roger began.

"Don't insult my intelligence," Cliff whispered harshly to Roger lest some first-class passenger overhear that thieves were making up a sizable chunk of the bellboy crew. "One of the other passengers saw you waiting for the men to leave. You've been caught red-handed."

Roger's face continued to turn a deeper shade of angry red. Dane almost felt sorry for him.

Cliff continued. "You're my responsibility until we get off the ship, unless I choose to have you thrown into the brig, which I don't have the heart to do. I guess you can continue to stay with us, but—"

"I don't need your charity," Roger snarled, whipping off his round bellboy hat and all but tossing it to Cliff. "I quit."

"What? What do you mean you quit! Where are you going to stay?" Cliff asked in disbelief.

"That's my business," Roger said haughtily, his soft,

wide shoulders arching proudly. I'll make do." He turned angrily and stalked off in the direction of the elevators, then turned and came back, getting close to Dane, who took a step back, ready to defend himself. Even though he was a few years older than Dane, he was the same height, but not the same weight. Dane figured Roger could squash him at will.

"You'd better watch your back," Roger muttered menacingly to Dane.

"You can't do anything to me," Dane replied, hoping he sounded more confident than he felt.

If it was possible Roger got even closer to Dane, so that their noses were almost touching. "You're on a sinking ship," he whispered, a look of grim satisfaction on his features.

"What?" Dane gasped, eyes wide and staring. Roger turned again and was gone.

Cliff, who had heard all of this, said to Dane, "Well, that certainly was interesting."

"What do you think he's gonna do now?" Dane questioned. He was only half curious; the other half was wrestling with what Roger had said about the sinking ship.

"I have no idea," Cliff answered as he watched Roger disappear through a doorway. "More than likely he'll need some time to cool off. When he realizes he doesn't have a place to stay tonight, he'll be back. I guess I'll let him sleep in our room, but with an attitude like that I'll be damned before I let him work with us again."

At last Dane stared down at the message he still had clutched in his hand. "I suppose I'll go deliver these now."

"Before you go, I must say to you that you did well."

"With what?"

"With this situation. Turning the wallet in, I mean. Especially considering your past history."

*Past history*, Dane thought as he groaned inwardly. Even though he was beaming inside at Cliff's compliment, he still hated his "past history" coming up. He disliked having something continually rearing its ugly head that he didn't actually do. Being put in someone else's shoes was really hard.

But Dane remained silent. No use in bringing all of this up with Cliff, so he just smiled and looked at his shoes instead.

"We'll be a bit short-handed with Roger gone," Cliff continued, "but I'll see what we can do about getting some time off for you tomorrow. As a reward."

"Time off? Tomorrow?" Dane said, amazed. He couldn't believe his good fortune. If he was to save his sister he was going to need all the time he could muster to get the job done. He didn't want to be spending the entire day on Sunday running messages around for passengers.

"Is that all right with you? Perhaps we can give you

tomorrow afternoon off."

"That would be great!" Dane exclaimed, not believing his good luck.

Cliff grinned. "All right, then. Better deliver that message."

"You're on a sinking ship," Roger had told Dane. These words had continued to bounce unceasingly through his mind as he delivered his message. Now, on his way back to Cliff, it came to him.

Roger knew. He had to know.

But how?

Dane's feet hustled over the red carpet as he neared his destination. His mind raced along with them, searching for an answer.

Roger had seen him earlier that morning as he had put the book in his duffel bag, hadn't he? Dane had caught him eyeing the bag.

"Great," Dane mumbled. All of a sudden, how much time he had off tomorrow didn't seem to matter. If he didn't have the book to show the captain, the ship might as well hit the iceberg right now. No captain worth his salt was going to listen to a ten-year-old thief of a bellboy without a whole lot of proof.

Deciding that delivering a message wasn't so important (even if it meant getting bawled out by Cliff), Dane bypassed the lounge in favor of the elevators again.

Upon reaching the bellboy room Dane conducted a quick search, but once again, no Roger.

Heart pounding, Dane crossed the room to his bunk and crouched down, then pulled his duffel bag from under the bunk and stared at the straps. How many lives hinged on whether or not a simple book was in this tan-colored bag?

Holding his breath, Dane opened the bag.

The book lay right where he had left it, the way he had left it. He sighed heavily with relief as he pulled out the book. The glare from the sun outside bounced off the slick cover, winking at him. He clutched it to his chest. He was positive now that Roger had not seen the book, or else it would be gone, stolen, a victim of Roger's sticky fingers.

Wouldn't it?

But the book wasn't safe. No way. He had to find a place where he could hide it, and it couldn't be anywhere near his bunk area.

But where? No loose floorboards or safes behind pictures popped out at him. So it had to be somewhere obvious.

Roger's bed, perhaps?

Dane cinched the straps of his duffle and carried the book to Roger's bed. If Roger had seen something in Dane's bag and wanted to search through it, he wouldn't find it because he was going to hide it…

Right under Roger's mattress.

# CHAPTER ELEVEN

Dane leaned heavily on the white rail that separated him from the freezing waters of the Atlantic Ocean, watching the wake of the ship disappear far behind in the darkness. The brisk April wind whipped against his face, chilling his nose and ears and turning them a deep shade of red. The tails of his brown overcoat flapped about his legs, the sound mixing and mingling with the noise of the *Titanic's* flag fluttering high overhead.

He sighed, tired but content. He brought his left arm up to his face wearily and punched the light button.

9:38 P.M.

He had worked from the time he had hid the book until six, when Cliff had collected him for dinner. From 6:45 P.M. until eight o'clock he had been trained on the elevators. Aaron had trained him so thoroughly and diligently that Dane had felt a pang of sadness course through him.

Aaron, of course, had trained Dane as if the bellboys would be operating elevators tomorrow, and the day after that, and the day after that. As if everyone on this ship had a future, which of course, very few of them did. Dane realized that he was taking it for granted that he knew the ship was going down. Aaron trained Dane well because he didn't have a clue what they were headed for only a little over twenty-four hours away. If he had known, he wouldn't have felt like training anyone. It made Dane sad when he remembered reading in one of the many *Titanic* books available (including the principal's) that none of the bellboys on this ship had lived to step on the rescue ship, *Carpathia*.

He belonged to a doomed brotherhood.

By the time eight o'clock had rolled around Dane had become an expert elevator operator under the watchful eye of his newfound friend. He had even been given the opportunity to give some of the *Titanic's* passengers a lift.

Ha ha.

Cliff had come around and relieved Dane and Aaron of their duties for the rest of the day, and Dane had been all but too happy to accept. It wasn't that he was lazy, but rather that he had never worked so hard in his whole entire life.

He had felt like he could just curl up in a corner of the elevator and go to sleep.

But after he had wound his way through endless corridors to his room, and had seen that no one was getting ready for bed, he discovered his second wind. Cliff, who was changing out of his uniform and not into pajamas but into regular street clothes, had informed Dane that as long as he was in bed by ten, he didn't have to turn in right that moment if he didn't want to. Dane had found an assortment of clothes in his duffel and had changed as well, ready to do something, just not sure what.

The bellboys and liftboys, now off duty, found many different ways of amusing themselves. Reading, playing cards, talking, walking the ship, writing letters home. Cliff had even brought back food to their room that he had liberated from the galley. As they ate together, joked and laughed, Dane felt his bond growing stronger and stronger with these boys, even though he had just met them this morning. He felt happy. Happy and content, even though he knew what was around the corner. He was choosing to enjoy the moment.

Now he was leaning over the rail of the ship, his breath frosting out in front of him. This was a nice way of wrapping up his day, a nice, quiet moment in a busy, bustling environment. Right before this he had walked various decks of the ship, his keys tucked in one of the pockets of his slightly oversized coat. Luckily, no officers questioned him about who he was and where he was going. They had just tipped their caps to him and given him a smile. He had felt free to walk where he wanted to walk and unlock whatever he wanted to unlock. He had stuck mostly to the crew areas and the third-class passenger berths. He would have been given too many odd looks if he had hung around the first-class sections wearing the clothes he was in.

9:45 P.M. Time to go.

He made his way back to his room right around ten and became part of the bellboy bedtime bustle. He smiled to himself. That sounded like some kind of old-fashioned dance from camp.

He changed into his pajamas and brushed his teeth. On his way back from the bathroom he cast a quick glance at Roger's bed.

"Yeah, weird, isn't it?" Cliff said, noticing Dane's look. "I'm afraid if I report it and the master-at-arms finds him, he'll be in hot water. I suppose I'll let it go, at least for tonight. What do you think?"

Dane shrugged. He hadn't actually given it too much thought; he was just glad that Roger wasn't around, giving him mischievous little looks. He hadn't missed him. "Sounds good to me," he said.

Cliff seemed satisfied as he stood near the light switch, ready to throw the room into darkness.

Dane's head hit the pillow and he smiled as he heard Abby's art project crackle.

He was exhausted. The lights went off and his eyes

shut down with them.

He felt like it was only a few seconds later when his shoulder was shaken. Only a few seconds of sleep and he was unwillingly being roused out of a thick, dark fog, a fog which he didn't want to leave. Trying to hide it he punched the light button on his watch.

Exactly twelve o'clock.

Twelve o'clock? Twelve o'clock of what day? What day was it? Saturday? Sunday? Was the ship sinking? Was it Sunday night? Had he messed the whole thing up?

"It's me, Cliff," a voice said from the darkness. "Are you awake?"

"What day is it?" Dane asked quickly, the panic enveloping him.

"Sunday. It just turned Sunday."

Dane, coming further out of his fog, breathed a jagged sigh of relief.

"What was that light?" Cliff questioned.

"A small torch," Dane said, remembering the English word for flashlight.

"Oh. I've never seen one so—"

Dane purposely cut him off. "Is something wrong?"

"No," Cliff responded. "Some of us are going on a little excursion. Want to come?"

Dane, now fully awake from the shaking of his shoulder and the pounding of his heart, asked, "Where?"

"It's a surprise. If you want to come, get dressed quietly. Not everyone is awake. Welcome to the select few."

His curiosity now aroused, Dane shook off the covers and his pajamas and groped in the near pitch black for his clothes. If it hadn't been for the light from the hallway coming in under the door, Dane might have been searching for his clothes for the next half hour.

Fully dressed, Dane met Cliff and a few others he couldn't see at the door. Cliff cracked it, peered cautiously out like a small animal making sure there were no predators, and then ushered them into the hall. The four boys followed Cliff (who, like the others, was now in his street clothes) as he led them down a flight of stairs to F Deck. Even though there was no one to be seen, Dane glanced to and fro nervously as he followed the others, on the lookout for someone who would see them and do...whatever it was they would do.

He couldn't afford to get into trouble right now, but he had to admit this was exciting.

As if reading his mind, Aaron, the liftboy, whispered, "Fun, ain't it?"

"Yeah!" Dane whispered back. "Where are we going?"

"Ah! You'll see!" Aaron replied, smiling.

Then Dane was ushered by the rest of the boys into a dim room amongst a volley of nervous giggles and laughs and harsh whispers. He didn't know where he was, having missed the sign on the door. It smelled slightly like a locker room, but he couldn't be sure. The door was shut behind them.

"Boy, that was lucky, Cliff," a boy named Simon said. "Last night we almost got caught. No one's out tonight."

Cliff grunted at the sixteen-year-old. "We did get lucky. There's almost always someone walking about."

"What are we doing?" Dane finally dared to ask.

"Swimming!" Aaron replied.

## CHAPTER TWELVE

"Swimming?" Dane repeated.

"Yeah, swimming," Cliff said. "Didn't you know the *Titanic* had a pool?"

Of course Dane knew this, how could he not? The *Titanic*'s pool was one of the newest and grandest features of the ship of dreams. Who didn't know about the pool?

Choosing to play dumb, he just shrugged. A survey of his surroundings showed him that they were in a men's changing room, not unlike others he had been to in gyms and pools. Wood benches were anchored to the green floor, and hangers and bins to hang clothes and place shoes in lined the walls.

"We're not allowed to use it," Cliff went on with a sarcastic smirk. "Only the first-class. Being that this is extremely unfair, we are fixing this situation at the only time possible."

The other boys laughed as they began to take off their clothes, their voices thin and echoey in the green tiled room.

"What do I swim in?" Dane asked as he joined them.

"Usually nothing," Cliff said. He pointed to a rack that had suits hanging on it. "But tonight, you'll want to wear one of those. We have lady friends joining us."

There were a few snickers from Aaron and Simon and another boy who had introduced himself to Dane in the hall as Alfred.

"Lady friends?"

"Girls," Aaron drawled sarcastically, tugging off his shirt. "Cliff invited some of his waitress friends to join us." He snickered again.

"Oh," Dane said, and continued pulling off his clothes. He walked over to the rack Cliff had pointed out and selected a suit, a funny looking thing that looked like a tank top that had been melded to a pair of biking shorts. He pulled off his watch and hid it in his pants pocket. No sense in getting it water damaged, even though it said waterproof. If it broke, where would he go to get a replacement? He figured the ship's gift shop didn't sell digital watches.

The five boys exited the changing area and entered the pool room. As they did Dane breathed a sigh of contentment. He was on top of the world. There was a hard day's work behind him, he was breaking stupid rules and getting away with it, and he was about to frolic in the ship's pool with gorgeous ladies.

Life was good.

The five entered and Dane realized suddenly how spoiled he was by the swimming pools he had been to at various gyms and water parks. Whereas the *Titanic* was gargantuan in size, the pool was not. He supposed the ship's passengers were lucky to have a pool at all, since this was a relatively new development in the history of shipbuilding.

Nonetheless, it was still a pool, and they had it to themselves.

In the daytime the saltwater pool would have been lit by natural light flooding in through the circular windows, but Cliff explained to Dane that he wasn't about to turn on the pool lights for fear of attracting late night ship walkers. He chose instead to turn on the locker room light (something he thought was risky as well, but better than the alternative) and crack the door into the pool.

Dane couldn't imagine anyone walking the ship this late at night, but didn't say anything.

He grabbed a towel from a stand, tossed it on a small bench nearby and then slipped quietly into the dark seawater, sucking in his breath as he did. The water was cold, but not unbearable. He pushed off the ladder with his feet and glided through the water, feeling carefree. He knew it wouldn't last long, but he was going to exploit every minute of this and enjoy it while it lasted.

He bumped into Aaron, who had entered the pool on the other side, and then was nearly squashed by Alfred who did a rather noisy cannonball and was shushed by Cliff. For the first five minutes they continually glanced at the entrance to the pool, but when no one showed up they began to let their guard down and make more commotion. Cliff didn't mind too much, saying that the pool was probably soundproofed.

They all held their breath momentarily when the door cracked open from the women's locker room, spilling white light across the pool. Collectively they let it out when it turned out to be Cliff's promised guests. The ladies closed the door behind them and slipped into the pool, wearing suits that even in the dark Dane could tell were not that different from what he was wearing.

Equally ugly and strange.

Now there were ten of them. Unconsciously they all came together in the center of the pool, and Cliff, who seemed to know all of them, introduced Dane to each in turn. "This is Violet, Margaret, Ann, Mary, and Louise." They each nodded and said hello politely. Dane nodded in greeting and said hello to each, happy at this latest addition of friends.

He was feeling less and less alone as this day progressed, which made him feel good. On the other hand, it began to gnaw at him that he was on the *Titanic* and spending time with people. Every time he had read about the *Titanic* he had always glossed over the number of deaths on this ship as if they were merely tally marks. He was beginning to realize what a tragedy the *Titanic* had been (was going to be). He was now able to actually see the people behind the statistics.

For the next half hour they swam, talked, joked, and splashed in the marble pool. Even Cliff, who had been nervous at first, had loosened up and joined the fun and ceased to shush them all. For a while, at least, Dane found it easy to forget that if he weren't able to do anything this pool would hold a lot more water as of tomorrow night.

In the gloom Dane noticed a lady getting out. He saw that she was a little heavier than the rest and moved a bit slower. Curious, he swam over to Cliff, who was busy trying to dunk Violet, and asked him who it was.

"Oh, that's Margaret," Cliff replied as he dodged a slap from Violet. "She's one of the first-class passengers who made friends with Violet here."

"She's very nice," the girl named Violet replied. "Go say hello."

Dane thought he might do just that. There was something that he thought he recognized, even in the blue darkness of the pool. And the fact that Cliff had said she was a first-class passenger...

Could it possibly be?

Dane swam to the edge of the pool and hoisted himself out, then sat next to the woman, who was occupying one of the only benches in the place.

"Excuse me, you're sitting on my towel," he said.

"Oh, I'm sorry," the woman apologized as she stood enough for Dane to give it a tug. "My name is Mrs. J. J. Brown," she said in a twangy Midwest accent, holding out her hand. "My friends call me Margaret. Who are you?"

"Dane," he replied, shaking her hand with one of his and toweling off his hair with the other.

"Dane, huh? Interesting name. Do you work on the ship, Dane?"

"Yes, ma'am, I do." He said politely. "I'm one of the bellboys." Then he asked the question that would spill her identity to him. "Where are you from?"

"I'm on my way home to Denver," she replied. "It's been awhile since I've been home."

Dane smiled in the dark. He had thought so. He was talking to the famous Molly Brown, heroine of the *Titanic*. "I'm from Colorado myself," he said.

"What part?"

"Silver Rush."

"Never heard of it."

"It's not too far from Denver."

"Still never heard of it."

Dane grinned at her. She was every bit as fiery as the history books and movies portrayed her to be. He was taking a strong liking to her with each passing moment.

"Why are you here at the pool this late?" he questioned.

"Just look at me," she said, sitting up tall, still toweling her head. "Would you want to go swimming with a bunch of other women looking the way I do? This is the only time I could come when I wasn't being gawked at by a bunch of first-class women. My friend Violet arranged for this little private pool party for this old lady."

"You're not old."

Margaret Brown slapped Dane hard on the arm. "You sure do know how to win an old lady over," she laughed, her voice echoing loudly in the pool room, making Dane afraid that the *Titanic* police would arrive in force and throw them all in the brig. Oh well. If they hadn't shown up yet, they probably wouldn't.

"Aren't you a prize," Margaret continued. "You'll make some lady happy."

"I mean it," he said. "I don't think you're old, anyway."

"Well sir, I appreciate that." Then, changing the subject, she said, "So what do you think of this floating palace we're on?"

And just how was Dane supposed to answer that bomb of a question?

Excited? Yes.

Apprehensive? Yes.

Fearful? Yes.

Before he could answer she started up again. "Yes sir, I've never been on an unsinkable ship before. And this one doesn't even look like a tank, does it? This is a nice ship."

"What if it's not unsinkable?" Dane ventured, toweling off his legs nonchalantly as she glared at him with a mixture of curiosity and suspicion, but with humor in her eyes as well.

"Funny you should say that. I've been wondering about that myself. I mean, how do you make a ship unsinkable? I guess if you blow a hole in it big enough, it would go down, right?"

"Or if it hit an iceberg," Dane added.

"Right. Then what would happen?"

"I guess we'd go down," he said, dropping the towel on the bench next to him. "What would you do if that happened?"

"I guess I'd get on a lifeboat with everyone else."

"But what if there weren't enough?" he asked. He knew that tomorrow night, if the ship did hit the iceberg, she would be one of the passengers to be ushered onto a lifeboat, but he pressed his question anyway, curious to know what she would do if pushed in a corner.

"Enough what?"

"Enough lifeboats."

"Of course there are enough lifeboats," she retorted.

"Have you counted? There aren't enough for all the people on this ship."

"How do you know that?"

"Simple math."

Margaret looked curiously at him again. It occurred to Dane that she hadn't yet met a member of the ship's crew who was this edgy about the ship he worked on.

"I'd stay on board, then, and let others fill those lifeboats, I suppose. I can go down with the best men around."

"But you can't!" Dane nearly shouted as he jumped off the bench, his voice echoing and drawing some quick glances from the pool hoppers. He lowered it as he said, "You have to get on."

Margaret watched his outburst with only a smile as she toweled off her legs, as if used to seeing emotional people. "Why? I can pull my weight as well as any man. Even more!" she laughed, making fun of herself. "I'd help load boats, or do anything else—"

"But you would be needed on the lifeboats!" Dane argued, still standing. His mind whirled in panic. How was he going to make her understand she was needed? History would be rewritten if she were to stay. Dane knew of her heroics on the lifeboat. He knew that she had helped to row, and boost the morale of the other passengers. What would happen if she went down with the ship?

Had he said too much now that she was aware of the numbers of people?

"What are you talking about, Dane? You're acting like we're about to have an accident."

Dane sat down again, trying to appear calm. He had almost given away more than he had intended. "It just seems to me that you would be useful to crew members on the lifeboats, that's all." He tried to make his voice sound normal and indifferent, and knew he was failing miserably.

"I guess we'll never know, will we?" she asked Dane. "Well, this old gal has got to go and stop spending time with young bucks like yourself." Margaret stuck her hand out again and Dane shook it. He felt a little star struck as he did so; it wasn't everyday that one got to hang around and shake hands with a famous heroine who had her own museum in Denver.

"I'll see you later," Dane said.

"Sure," Margaret said with a friendly smile. "Maybe I'll see you swimming again tomorrow night."

*That might be more true than you know,* Dane thought dismally. If he failed, he would be doing the swimming.

"Maybe," he said, again trying to sound cheerful.

But he didn't feel it.

It was around one-thirty when the five returned to their room. In the cloying darkness Dane changed ungracefully back into his pajamas and tumbled into bed, now even more exhausted than he had been a few hours earlier. He wondered briefly how he was going to feel at seven when Cliff roused them all. It probably hadn't been the best idea to stay up this late the night before what he was sure would be the biggest and most challenging day and night of his life.

But what could he do now? The best answer was to fall asleep, and in less than two minutes, he had.

# CHAPTER THIRTEEN

Dane walked down the hallway toward his breakfast on Sunday morning, feeling like this day had begun in much the same fashion as yesterday. It would be hard for him to forget that it was The Fateful Sunday, even if he had wanted to.

Which he did.

What he wouldn't give right now to spend this morning warm and curled up into a ball in his bed at home. No worries, no cares. The butterflies flying around in his stomach made him doubt that he would be able to choke down any oatmeal. The thought of eating when forced with the awesome challenges he most certainly would face today made him want to throw up, and he hadn't even eaten anything.

But he ate anyway, knowing that he had no choice, that he needed his energy, as his mom would say. He wondered fleetingly if prison inmates on death row felt the same as he did on the morning of their execution.

Probably not, but it had to be close.

The morning passed quickly and without much fanfare. He was pleased that Cliff had put him on duty as a liftboy rather than asking him to run around the ship delivering messages. He would need to conserve energy; he figured he might be doing plenty of dashing about the ship later in the day.

As he threw the switch back and forth for passengers, he formed a plan in his head.

Finish work.

Lunch.

The rest of the day off, thanks to Cliff.

Visit Abby again, a move which she was not expecting but would be pleased with, he was sure.

Retrieve the book from Roger's bed and show it to Captain Smith.

Save the ship.

Take a swim in the pool to celebrate the fact that the *Titanic* was not on the bottom of the North Atlantic.

Yes sir, he had his day pretty well planned out. He supposed that he should try to get the book to Captain Smith as quickly as he could, indeed, he probably should have shown it to him already. But Dane hadn't wanted to bring out the book too quickly since everyone would want to look at it.

Captain Smith would probably show it to too many officers for a second opinion if he had too much time on his hands. Dane felt it was for the captain's eyes only, and even then should only be brought out as a precautionary measure. Dane would like to just talk with the captain first, and then show the book to confirm his story. Besides, he didn't even know where the captain was right at the moment, anyway. He knew that shortly before the *Titanic's* collision, Smith had retired for the evening inside his cabin.

This was Dane's next move. To catch the captain in his room, and that would be shortly after nine o'clock. 9:20 P.M., to be exact. That would give him a couple of hours to reason with the captain.

Until then he had some time to kill and would try his best to keep the butterflies in his stomach down to a dull roar. It didn't seem fair that everyone else on this ship was having a fine Sunday morning. Some were walking the deck, some were eating, and some were resting; all without a care in the world as they floated toward America on the grandest ship ever built. And here he was, very much aware of what might happen this evening.

"Got to try and stay calm," he muttered to himself as an elderly first-class passenger and his wife stepped onto the elevator and ordered him to go down to C Deck.

He threw the lever, and down they rattled.

The rest of the morning came and went without incident. Cliff had dismissed Dane for the rest of the afternoon as promised and Dane had lunch in the same lifeboat he had been in yesterday, this time without Cliff, who had gotten sidetracked in helping a first-class passenger track down a friend in second-class.

There had been no sign of Roger, which was beginning to creep Dane out. He didn't hold a soft spot in his heart for him, of that he was certain. And he didn't miss the older boy skulking around in his pouting manner, looking for something to meddle in. It interested Dane that he had known Roger for just a little over a day, and in that time they had both fostered an intense dislike for each other. He supposed that just happened with some people. For no particular reason some people just didn't hit it off too well.

Dane had to admit that he would rather have Roger around than not having any clue to his whereabouts. The rest of the bellboys were largely ignoring Roger's disappearance; Dane assumed that no one cared for him very much. But not having him in plain sight was like a mouse not knowing exactly where the lurking cat was.

The longer Roger stayed away, the more Dane was beginning to feel like the mouse. Roger had left, largely because of what Dane had done, and now not seeing Roger was even worse than seeing him.

After a lunch of sardine sandwiches (they were actually pretty good) Dane retraced yesterday's path to third-class. His pounding on her door went unanswered by Mrs. Arthur and he wondered what had happened to her when a young woman in a faded green dress and a French accent spotted him. She explained to Dane that Mr. Arthur and his group of boys was visiting Mrs. Arthur and her girls in the third-class lounge several decks up. He thanked her, and with his keys clanking against his leg started the journey to the lounge just underneath the poop deck. As he neared the lounge he heard people talking, laughing, singing, and generally enjoying themselves. Even though he liked the first-class areas, he thought that being a third-class passenger would probably have been closer to his liking. The people in third-class seemed lighter hearted, despite the fact that their lives must be much harder than their first-class counterparts.

The lounge was busy, although he was sure it wasn't nearly as full as it was on most nights. Some people had eaten and gone for a nap, but others were socializing. He didn't know how long he had spent looking for her in this crowd, but when he did spot her she had already seen him and was running toward him, arms outstretched, her ragged rabbit doll flopping in her hand.

He had been allowed his watch, she her stuffed rabbit named Henry that had accompanied her to Dane's house.

If only she had been allowed to bring a helicopter.

Two hours later Dane left the third-class lounge, a

grin on his sweaty, red face. During his time there he had played games such as tag and hopscotch with the other orphans, quite unaware of the passage of time. Let it pass, for all I care, he had thought. At the moment, anyway, he had nothing better to do. If anything, his time with his sister had helped to relieve his mind of its heavy burden.

Dane and Abby hadn't spoken much about the upcoming evening, other than to briefly review the plan they had made the day before. If the ship hit the iceberg Dane would come and get her. If the ship didn't hit, he would try to visit her anyway to tell her everything was okay so she didn't stay awake all night worrying.

Other than that, he had just had fun with her. Bonding time. He had hated to go, and the other orphans (who seemed to know him, wasn't that strange!) had clung to him and protested his having to leave them. But he wanted to check and make sure his *Titanic* book was where he had left it, so he pulled away from them as gently as possible. He had never felt such love and admiration as he had at that moment, and he had to admit that he liked it. He liked it a lot.

He was whistling to himself and his mind was a million miles away as he walked his way back to the room when he sensed someone behind him. As he turned to see who it was, he felt something slam into the back of his head, hard. The last thing he remembered before darkness overtook him was the image of Roger, towering over him, a leer of satisfaction stretched over his face.

And then it was lights out.

# CHAPTER FOURTEEN

Darkness and pain.

As Dane groggily peeled his eyelids apart (feeling every bit like they had been sealed together with Super Glue), his first thought was that he had gone blind. He opened and shut them a few times rapidly, and not being able to tell a difference, began to panic.

Dane remembered the not-so-nice image of Roger leering down at him, some object held in his thick hand.

*Great*, thought Dane. *He hit me over the head and now I'm blind. I'm lying in the Titanic's hospital room and I've gone completely blind. If my dad weren't about forty-five years away from being born, he'd really want to sue somebody.*

But if he was in a hospital room, why did it feel like his feet were straight up in the air?

Dane pulled his feet down (it felt like they were

propped up against a wall, that was weird…) and struggled unsteadily to a sitting position. He fought off the sudden urge that washed over him to throw up. The need subsided, thankfully. It wouldn't be a pretty sight if he barfed all over the *Titanic's* pretty nurses.

Not that he would be able to see it.

*These beds sure are uncomfortable,* he thought as he felt the bed. But it wasn't a bed. It was the floor.

He leaned forward and touched what his feet had been propped up against.

It had been a wall.

This wasn't a hospital! It felt more like a closet!

He hit the light button on his watch, and into the pitch black sprung a dim glow. He sighed a deep breath of relief. At least he wasn't blind.

The watch light was no high-powered flashlight, but it shed enough light so that he could get a handle on his situation.

Yep. It was a closet. And that tender lump on the back of his head that was a gift from Roger was throbbing like mad.

That wasn't fair. After getting hit in the head, wasn't the hero supposed to end up in the hospital, being taken care of by pretty nurses? Instead he had been crammed into a closet not much bigger than himself. Holding his hands out perpendicular from himself, he discovered he could touch the wall on either side. After some more grop-ing around he felt some wooden poles, and then followed the length down to their bristly end.

Brooms.

He was in a broom closet. How glamorous for the hero of the *Titanic*. He would have to forgo the act of be-ing worshipped and revered because of his attempts in the near future to save the ship.

He was cooped up in a closet with a bunch of brooms.

He hit the light button on his watch again. The blue light revealed the brooms, a mop, and him. It was then that he realized he didn't even know where he was on the ship. He could be anywhere that the rat Roger had the whim to take him.

He stood unsteadily on his feet, finding it hard to keep his balance because of the blow to his head and the intense dark. It reminded him of the time at school when his P.E. teacher had made them pull one leg up behind them and try to keep their balance. It hadn't been too difficult until the teacher had told them to do it with their eyes closed, and then there had been a rainfall of students as they had lost their balance and pitched onto the floor.

"And what is the lesson?" the P.E. teacher had asked.

We use our eyes for balance, as well as to see with. That had been the lesson. Dane understood that even better now as he leaned against the wall and attempted not to keel over against the brooms.

Feeling in the air in front of him like a blind man searching for something, Dane hunted for the doorknob of the closet. When his hands came into clumsy contact with it he tried to turn it and found it (of course) unmovable.

He guessed he wasn't surprised. Roger wouldn't have taken the precious time to knock Dane out and detain him in an unlocked closet, now would he? He might be mean and surly, but stupid he wasn't. Dane wondered if Roger had spent the night holed up in a closet like this one, biding his time until the moment presented itself to give his no good enemy a whack over the head.

Wondering for the first time what time it was (it couldn't be that late; it felt like Roger had just a few moments ago given him a headache to go with the rest of his problems) he hit the light button again.

8:23 P.M.

"Eight twenty-three!" Dane exclaimed, barely noticing the way his loud voice sounded in the confined space. What had happened to the time? He quickly estimated that he had been "out of commission" for about five hours. The blow to his head and the late night out last night had really taken its toll on him.

Dane felt his stomach drop as if it were lined with lead. The feeling of wanting to vomit returned. Once again he pushed it away as he continued to steady himself against the smooth closet wall.

This was no time to puke or pass out. He had to keep his head about him, no matter how late it was.

Dane grabbed the knob again and twisted it hard, then put his shoulder against it, braced one of his feet against the far closet wall, and pushed.

Still nothing.

"Is anybody out there?" he called tentatively as he banged on the door. Again his voice sounded loud in the enclosed space, but he knew his voice hadn't carried very far.

The only answer to his query was a dull, throbbing silence punctuated with what he imagined to be the thumping and humming of the *Titanic's* engines. He felt suddenly suffocated by the closet and was grateful for not being scared of the dark or of tight, enclosed spaces. Was this what someone buried alive would feel like? Trapped in a dark, enclosed coffin with no one to hear them scream? Surely this is what it felt like, minus the maggots.

*He* had brooms.

Dane banged his fist against the door and hollered louder, then experimented with a few hard kicks to the bottom of the door as he yelled, "Hey! Is there anyone out there?"

Deciding this approach was lacking in effectiveness he backed himself up against the back wall of the closet and kicked out with all his might with his right foot.

The door hardly even shuddered, just stood solidly upright and defied him. He tried it again, but the response was the same. The door to his tomb remained solid and steadfastly unyielding. Disappointment mingled with panic as he envisioned being in there for four hours, five hours, six… He imagined water pouring in through the thin crack at the bottom as he tilted sideways, air being forced out of the closet, and eventually his lungs. Not to mention what would happen to Abby. He imagined her sitting quietly on a bunk in her room, hands clasped around her rag doll, waiting for him, refusing everyone's pleas to try to make it up to the Boat Deck. Waiting for her big brother because, after all, he did say if this happened he would come and get her, and she trusted him.

He had to get out of here.

He began repeatedly to kick the door and hammer on it with his fists. He yelled for help. He jiggled and twisted and fought with the stubborn doorknob.

Nothing. Still.

He looked at his watch. He continued glancing at it as time frantically raced by.

Eight forty-five.

Nine o'clock.

Ten o'clock.

Ten-thirty.

Eleven o'clock.

# CHAPTER FIFTEEN

Cliff walked briskly over the *Titanic's* thick hallway carpet of the first-class section on B Deck, his eyes frantically
searching. He scanned adjacent hallways and corners. He
walked by B52, B54, B56, peering into doors briefly if they
were open and rushing by hurriedly if they were not. B102.
Hallway. B104. No sign of him.

His face was pale and sweat was leaking its way to the
collar of his uniform. His stride was strong because he was
in a rush, but if he were to stand still his legs would shake
noticeably. His breath was coming in and out in harsh
rasps. He had been all over the blasted ship looking for a
boy. The boy, who held the answers to his myriad of questions that were all piling together and running over, was
missing.

In Cliff's sweaty left hand he grasped a book. He kept
the book palmed against his leg, as if to shield it from the

prying eyes of nosey passengers. If one was trying to be extra nosey, however, an intensely observant glance might get them a title.

*The Life and Death of the Titanic*, it would say.

Cliff's legs were threatening to give out on him between the combination of nervousness and their ever-increasing activity. As time inched past on the watch he carried in his pocket, the intensity of his search increased. He jumped at every shadow, every movement, and every person, especially if that person were a boy.

Where, oh where, was Roger?

If he could find him, it might answer a lot of questions. So far, though, his search had turned up nothing. Snatching at his watch, he saw that it now read 9:45 P.M. Where had the time gone?

Cliff's day had been mostly normal up until dinnertime. Sunday was a slow day on a ship for passing notes amongst passengers. Instead, they resorted to napping, playing cards, gambling, reading, or just walking the boat's decks. Cliff's previous bellboy crews on other ships were usually able to catch a breath on Sundays, and today wasn't an exception, even though the one boy had time to himself for good behavior and one had disappeared almost entirely. It was almost like he had done a swan dive off the ship and vanished without a trace.

Cliff himself had been able to hand off his table watching duties to Aaron for a half hour while he catnapped on a lounge chair on the deck in the brisk April day.

Cliff had given Dane the rest of the day off and wasn't a bit surprised that he hadn't seen him all day. Dane had mentioned in passing that after lunch he was off to visit his sister, and Cliff figured that he probably even wrangled a way to have dinner with her, something that Cliff approved of. He had a girlfriend in England that he was courting between stints on the White Star Line, and someday he meant to marry her and raise kids of his own. Then he would spend as much time with them as he could, whenever he wasn't at sea, anyway. Spending time with his family was something he was sure he would hold dear.

Roger, on the other hand, was another issue. The boy was strange to him, strange and slightly devious. You could tell by looking in his eyes that something was lurking behind them. It was as if he was observing, waiting, and biding time. Cliff hadn't looked for an excuse to relieve Roger of his duty, partly because another member of the White Star Line besides Cliff had hired Roger, and partly because he couldn't think of any grounds to dismiss him. Although Roger looked like a snake that was sneaking up on a rat, it wasn't a basis to fire him.

And then Roger had made his own bed, so to speak, by being caught red-handed. Cliff hadn't reported the incident, at least not yet. He didn't want to get him in any more trouble than necessary, even though he didn't care for him much. Then Roger had made things worse by disappearing and not telling Cliff where he was or what he was up to.

"I wash my hands of him," Cliff had muttered to himself after dinner when he had failed to see Roger amongst the crew. Yes, he had made his own bed, and Cliff was going to unmake it.

And that's just what he had done after supper. He had departed the crew galley shortly after seven and gone into the bellboy's quarters. There he had proceeded to pack up in a large canvas bag all of Roger's belongings, perhaps later to be placed in the lost and found, or if he were in a real foul mood, thrown off the side of the ship and buried at sea. Cliff had been quite thorough as he cleaned up after Roger, and when he had lifted Roger's mattress to strip off the sheets...

The rest was, as they say, history.

Cliff had sat on the bunk underneath Roger's for the next half hour, pouring over the thick, colorful volume. At first his hands had remained steady, but as time passed they began to shake uncontrollably. Initially he thought the book had been printed up as a souvenir pictorial for passengers and he just hadn't seen it yet. That notion faded as he saw the underwater pictures of the wreckage and the photographs of people he knew with the word "deceased" written under them.

"What kind of prank is this?" he had mumbled as he flipped to the front to see the copyright date. 2007? Ninety-five years into the future? If this was a hoax, it was too well done.

And then there had been the picture of the bellboys, the photograph of himself and his crew. "All perished", the caption had read.

In the pit of Cliff's stomach a little creature named fear sunk its teeth in and began to gnaw away. Could this be true? The answer, he felt, lay with the owner of the book, which obviously was Roger.

Unsteadily Cliff had stood, pulling himself up using the bunk post.

He would have to find him, and by the look of the book and the date, soon.

His search had led him all over the ship. Through the gym, The Café Parisian, the Verandah and Palm Court, the second-class library, the maids' and valets' saloons.

No sign of him. His search had turned up nothing. Now he found himself going through the first-class area, hoping that he would catch sight of Roger. Perhaps a rich first-class passenger with pity on thieving bellboys had taken him in.

Doubtful, but who knew?

Alas, this search proved fruitless as well and at last he returned to his table in the first-class lounge. Presently it was being lorded over by Simon, one of the senior bellboys. His dark hair was thickly plastered to his skull with lard so that it gleamed across the expansive room. He had his hands behind his head and was leaning back in his chair, his hat resting on the table.

Simon glanced at the clock next to his hat. "You're late—" he began, but was cut off.

"We need to find Roger right away," Cliff began breathlessly. "We're going to need to get all the bellboys—"

It was Simon's turn to interrupt. "I saw him. On my way to my shift here."

Cliff's heart jumped. "You saw him?" he asked, anxiously. He had spent God knew how much time in his search and Simon had found him loitering around the ship, probably by accident.

"Taking Dane to hospital," Simon added.

"Taking Dane to hospital?" Cliff repeated, his eyebrows shooting to the ceiling.

"Yes, you know, it's on D Deck next to the second-class dining—"

"I know where it is!" Cliff snapped, almost taking the younger boy's head off. "What's wrong with Dane?"

"Roger said something about food poisoning. It looked like he could hardly stand up. Roger was just about dragging him."

Something gave a tug at Cliff, filling him with dread.

There was something about that last statement that Cliff didn't like at all.

"Food poisoning?" Cliff grilled.

"Food poisoning," Simon affirmed. "I didn't think the food here was that bad," he added with a grin.

What was Roger up to? Cliff wondered as he spun around to head for the infirmary, almost stumbling into a tall woman in an even taller hat. Now for some reason it seemed even more important to reach Roger. He had no idea as to who Roger really was, but as the owner of the book he had a lot of explaining to do. Cliff had to know if what happened to the *Titanic* on those pages was real, or if the whole thing was an elaborate hoax.

"What's going on?" Simon called out to Cliff's back.

Cliff turned as he walked backwards. "Can't tell you now. I'll fill you in later."

"Perhaps tonight while we're swimming?"

Cliff had a sudden and brief image of himself and others floundering about in the ice strewn waters of the Atlantic, the ship going down before their very eyes. Swimming, but not in a pool.

"Yeah, sure," he said, trepidation filling his voice.

He turned again. Time to hunt down Roger and Dane.

# CHAPTER SIXTEEN

Cliff left the hospital on D Deck and leaned against the wall in the hallway.

Now what was he going to do?

The trip had proved to be a waste of valuable time. Nurse Bannock was on duty, and she relayed to Cliff that the only patient she had seen was a second-class girl who had gotten two splinters in her hand. Dane who? Roger who? She wasn't familiar with either of those boys.

A quick glance at his pocket watch revealed that it was ten-thirty, and he was no nearer to solving this than he had been at seven-thirty when he had first found the accursed book.

There was a line from the book that he couldn't shake, no matter how much he tried. The sentence had followed him around this city of a ship, and now it cornered and surrounded him as he leaned helplessly and breathlessly against the wall. It taunted and teased him.

"No bellboys survived."

Roger really *was* on his way to the infirmary this time. The first time he had been seen in the hall by his mate Simon he had to come up with a lie, and quick. Even though he was dragging Dane to a secure closet on the deck below G Deck (which was called the Orlop Deck) he had told Simon that Dane had a wicked case of food poisoning from some bad sardines. Simon, obviously on his way back to Cliff after having delivered a message to a third-class passenger on B Deck, hadn't seemed to pay much attention. He had only given Roger a cursory glance and had continued on his way. Roger had towed Dane the rest of the way down the steps, Dane's feet dragging and thumping down corridors and stairs behind them. Toward the end of his journey, as he neared the closet he had been holed up in since yesterday afternoon, he had fallen down the last part of a flight of steps and had landed heavily on his knee, which had swollen to the size of a grapefruit.

He had unlocked the closet door with a key (he hadn't felt like turning over his ring of keys yet, thank you very much) and tossed Dane inside. That would teach him to meddle in other people's business, wouldn't it? He was not sure how long he would leave Dane in his dark cell, but he knew it would be a good long while. Dane was secure enough in the depths of the ship so as to not be found for a nice length of time, of that Roger was sure.

Roger had roamed the ship for a while, mostly staying out of people's sight. At last his knee screamed so loud for attention that he had limped off to hospital, hoping for some ice to take the swelling down.

As he neared the door he stopped dead in his tracks at the sight of his former boss. Cliff was leaning up against a wall, looking haggard. Roger tried to step around a corner without being seen, but it was too late. Cliff, now looking more elated than haggard, gave chase. It was no match. In a matter of seconds Cliff had snagged Roger's uniform (he hadn't bothered changing out of his work clothes) and had thrown him up against a wall.

"What?" Roger asked, trying his best to look annoyed.

"You have a lot of explaining to do, haven't you?" Cliff asked gruffly.

"I don't know—"

"Oh, let's not even start that," Cliff cut in. "First of all, what's this?" He lifted up the book and waved it about an inch away from Roger's face.

"I don't know. How about a book?" the boy answered sarcastically.

"Of course it's a book. How did it get here? Is it yours?"

"I can't see what it says," Roger gasped. Cliff had grabbed him by the front of the collar near his neck and was twisting it, making Roger's breathing labored.

"You don't need to see. You know what it is, don't you?" Cliff asked with a twist of the collar. "I found it under your mattress. Thieving again?"

To Cliff's delight Roger actually seemed surprised. "It wasn't under my mattress. It was—"

He stopped himself short, realizing he had just trapped himself.

"Aha! So you have seen the book before?" Cliff pressed.

"No! I mean, yes, I saw it. But I didn't take it and put it under my mattress like you said. It was in Dane's bag. I saw it the first day he was here with us. He took it out—"

"Dane?" Cliff asked. What was with this twist?

"Yeah. He had the book, not me. I didn't know it was anything important. I didn't even know what it was. I just looked at it when he wasn't in the room. I probably should have taken it. Does it tell the future or something?"

Cliff tightened his grip on the boy. "Enough questions out of you. Where did you take Dane?"

Roger sighed resignedly. "Orlop. Near the refrigerated cargo. Hey, let go, will ya? I won't run. Honest."

Cliff released his grip and Roger settled against the wall, massaging his neck.

"This is his book? Where did he get it?" He looked down at the sweaty volume in his hands with a look of wonder. "Do you—"

But Roger had been banking on this moment and used it to his full advantage. As soon as Cliff had lowered his eyes, he was off like a cannonball at the circus, minus the smoke.

"Hey!" Cliff called out to the retreating figure. He dashed after him but Roger grabbed a rolling tray that had been left outside of a second-class doorway, and spun it toward his ex-boss. It caught Cliff at the waist and entangled his legs like a bowling ball settling on nothing but a strike. Cliff careened over noisily, and that was all the time Roger needed to complete his escape. The boy ran heavily and awkwardly away, not looking like a man on the lam, but like a penguin on the loose from a zookeeper.

*He waddles like a duck*, thought Cliff crazily. But it didn't matter, because Roger had beaten him. Cliff hoisted himself up and brushed off the crumbs and milk that had attached itself to his maroon uniform. He could go after the boy, but what would be the point? By now Roger could be around any number of twists and bends in this ship, and it would be just a waste of precious time as he tried to find Dane.

"What's all the ruckus?" Nurse Bannock asked, wringing her old hands in worry as she poked her head out the infirmary door. She looked like the kind of woman who felt like nothing was in order unless it was neat and quiet, tucked away, put on a shelf, and dusted. The author of perfection.

"Nothing to worry your head about, ma'am. Little scuffle."

Nurse Bannock grunted disapprovingly and retreated into her cave.

Cliff looked forlornly down the hall, grappling with his new problem.

*Where is Dane?* He wondered.

Under duress Roger had said Orlop. Was he lying? Cliff didn't know for sure, but he didn't have any better idea on where to look for him.

He began to move once again, his tired legs carrying him forward, deeper and deeper into the bowels of the monster ship to see if he could find himself a boy who held the key to what was about to happen within the next few hours.

# CHAPTER SEVENTEEN

As the crew and passengers of the *Titanic* cruised their way through the dark, icy waters, they had no way of knowing what lay in the near future. As their home away from home cut its way through the black water, having an accident was the furthest thing from everyone's mind. What occupied their lives at the moment was not much more than the fleeting dreams that life carried. Here and there the ship held pockets of activity. There were some people having midnight snacks, some playing poker, and some reading. Most passengers, if not sleeping, were enjoying the other pleasures the ship had to offer. It would have been vain to presume that anyone on board had known that death was traveling with them, ready to collect.

Almost everybody was clueless, except for four. Dane, Abby, Cliff, and Roger.

Dane sat in the corner of the closet, arms wrapped

around legs tucked to his chest, head on knees. He was exhausted, and his hands were cut, bruised and throbbing. His face was hot and the sweat mingled with tears that ran dirty tracks down his cheeks.

*It's not fair*, he thought. At least if he were running around trying to save the ship he would feel better, feel useful. He had bided his time carefully, planned, and thought things through. He hadn't wanted to show the book too early to those who needed to see it. Too much information, he had figured, could sometimes be a bad thing. He didn't want the *Titanic's* entire crew poring over the book, trying to foresee their future. It would have been better to just bring out the book at the most opportune moment.

And now he wished he *had* done something right away, had shown it to the Captain, consequences be darned. Because now here he was, locked in a broom closet, no closer to saving the ship than he had been the day before yesterday, back in Colorado. The ship was going to go down anyway, and he had known and hadn't done anything.

He had failed.

He grabbed at the ridiculous bellboy hat still on his head and ripped it off, snapping the string. More tears ran down his cheeks and he sniffed hard as he scrubbed them away furiously, feeling like a baby. But he was entitled to a good cry, wasn't he? The fate of thousands of people rested on his shoulders, and—

What was that?

He could have sworn it sounded like a voice. Not just a voice, but a voice calling his name.

Ignoring his cramped legs Dane staggered to his feet. Despite the pain in his raw fists he began to pound on the wooden door once again. His voice sounded harsh and scratchy as he bellowed, "I'm here! I'm in here!"

"Dane! Is that you?" the voice asked, coming nearer. It sounded like Cliff!

"Yes, it's me! You've gotta get me out of here!"

A moment later he heard the sound of keys jingling, then the latch shot back and Dane burst out of the closet like a jack-in-the-box.

"Are you okay? What—" Cliff began, then stopped as Dane spotted the book and snatched it from his hand and started wobbling down the hall, looking very much to Cliff like he had been drinking.

"You found it!" Dane called over his shoulder to Cliff. Under other circumstances he would have found it perturbing that someone had found his carefully hidden book, but he had no time right now to mull it over.

"Yeah! Hey, where are you going?"

"I've got to warn the Captain!"

Cliff ran to keep up with Dane, who was now finding his legs useful again and picking up speed. "So it's not a joke or prank?" he questioned.

"No. It's really going to happen. I've got to warn—"

"I know, but you're going the wrong way!"

Dane stopped and spun around without missing a beat. "*I don't even know where I am,*" he realized.

Ten minutes later they were on C Deck, both red faced and out of breath. They were tearing along at a strong clip, but the endless stairways and long passageways had taken their toll on their lungs. Dane held the book in his sweaty hand, the glossy cover by now ripped and wrinkled from the wear and tear. No longer was it in mint condition.

"Tell me what's going on again," Cliff gasped out. "It's hard to believe."

"It's hard for you to believe? Try being in my position," Dane wheezed back. Then explaining as quickly and as best he could, he continued.

"I'm from the future. I've been sent here as a punishment for being mean to my foster sister, who's also on the ship. I have to stop it from sinking or save her, whichever I can pull off."

"Sent here by whom?" Cliff asked, almost running into a crewmember that was dressed in white and carrying a tray of empty dishes.

"My principal. Of my school."

"Principal?"

Dane fought to find the word Cliff might recognize. "Headmaster," he said at last.

"Oh. That's an unbelievable story, and I'm not sure I would believe you if it weren't for the book. No offense."

"None taken. Yeah, it is something, isn't it?" Dane stole a look at his watch. 11:11 P.M. There was still time...

"It gave me the creeps," Cliff said, close on Dane's heels. "I read about my death. All of our deaths."

"That's what I'm trying to avoid," Dane said as they exited the hall they had been running down. Ahead of them lay the grand staircase. It wasn't overly large, but to Dane and Cliff's eyes it looked like a very high mountain. Both sets of legs were tired and quivery and didn't feel fit enough to fly up a set of stairs that appeared as daunting as it did.

But they flew up them anyway.

Up past C Deck, B Deck, A Deck, and finally onto the Boat Deck they ran. Dane felt like he was near exhaustion. If he had to run any more, he would collapse in a puddle on the floor.

"This way to the captain's quarters," Cliff said in a voice faint with fatigue. "He might be in there, or he—"

"He's there," Dane interrupted as he remembered his *Titanic* history. Captain Smith had retired for the night, leaving the ship to Second Officer Lightoller, and then to First

Officer Murdoch's capable, if not slightly flawed, leadership abilities. Dane had a moment to wonder what might have happened if anyone else besides Murdoch had been in command that night. He smiled grimly to himself as he thought that that sounded like a question a teacher might ask.

"What would have happened if…"

The two ran down the hall. After Cliff had pointed to the correct door, Dane rapped sharply four times with his arm, trying to save his injured hands some pain.

"Sir?" Cliff called out.

There was a mumble from inside that sounded like someone was just waking up. Then a clear voice spoke. "Yes?"

"Sir," Cliff continued. "This is Clifford Harris, the chief bellboy. I very much need to speak with you."

"Right now," Dane whispered to Cliff.

"Right now," Cliff urged through the door.

There was a moment's pause before the door was opened. A rather round, bearded face complete with tired eyes peered at them from the crack.

"Yes?" he said again.

Cliff looked at Dane for help, trying to find the words. Finally he said, "Captain, could we come in? This shouldn't take long, and it is of the utmost importance."

*That's an understatement*, Dane thought.

He looked at his watch, 11:27 P.M.

Not much time left now, but enough.

Instead of looking angry or put off, the captain opened the door wider and ushered the two in. Dane had figured that at such a late hour the two of them would have been in for a good yelling at or at the very least a scowl or two accompanied by a firm door slam, but they received neither.

The room that they were invited into was the Captain's sitting room. Needless to say it was elegant and sumptuous, just as one would assume the captain of such a grand ship would have. The carpet was thick and red, and pictures of the *Titanic* covered the wood paneled walls.

Captain Smith gestured to three chairs that sat next to a small table adorned with a reading lamp. "Shall we?" he asked.

Dane and Cliff moved quickly to the chairs. Dane was increasingly aware of the fleeting time.

"I don't know how to start," Dane began nervously, "so I'll just start. We're going to sink."

Captain Smith paused halfway down to his seat, absorbing this new nugget of information that had just been thrown to him. Then he completed the motion, setting his arms on the arms of the chair. Dane thought that the captain looked more like a grandfather than a captain at this moment. Sitting in the chair minus his captain's jacket and hat, he looked more like your average old man ready to play Santa Claus in a mall than the captain of the grandest ship around.

"I'm sorry. Say that again?" he said, giving Dane an impenetrable stare.

"This ship is going to hit an iceberg at 11:40 PM. First Officer Murdoch is on duty. He'll order the ship hard to starboard—"

"Wait, wait," Captain Smith protested. "You say the ship is going to have an accident?"

"Yes," Dane replied. "It's going—"

"You have to understand that I really am rather short on sleep," Captain Smith said as he stood up, as if to end the conversation. "You will forgive me if I don't want to follow along with your little joke. And you, Mr. Harris, should know better than this."

*The captain has returned*, Dane thought. No longer did he look like a tired old man, but more like a captain in charge.

Cliff stood as well, looking politely angry and defensive. "Sir, this is not a joke. You need, I mean, I feel you should listen to him."

"This isn't a joke?" the captain asked. "Then what exactly are the two of you up to?"

Dane laid the *Titanic* book on the table, deciding it was time to apply his secret weapon to the situation. "I'm from the future, the year two thousand and seven, to be exact. I don't have time to explain how I got here, but I did."

"I find that hard to believe," Captain Smith said, doubt etched in his voice.

"I knew you would. That's why I brought this." Dane slid the book across the table.

The captain looked at it, his curiosity aroused. "*The Life and Death of the Titanic*," he read. "*Destruction on a Grand Scale?*"

"Open it," Dane insisted as he gave the book a shove again.

The captain flipped the cover open and riffled half-heartedly through the book. "When did you say this was going to happen? If, indeed, it is going to happen?"

Dane looked at his watch. 11:27 P.M.

Still?

His watch had come to a standstill?

"It's supposed to happen around eleven-forty," he said, staring with confusion at the timepiece. "But my watch has said 11:27 P.M. for awhile now."

Captain Smith looked at a clock he had hanging on the wall that Dane had missed upon his arrival. "It's eleven thirty-nine now," he stated.

Dane looked desperately, with a sinking feeling in his gut, at the watch again. The thing still said 11:27 P.M. The seconds were frozen at twenty-eight. It must have been jolted somehow on the way up.

"You have to go up to the bridge now!" Dane shouted

as he jumped out of the chair, his eyes wide. "Murdoch won't steer the ship correctly!"

Captain Smith lifted the book off the table and thumbed through it, slower this time. "I see no reason to get yourself excited. Mr. Murdoch is a very capable man, and I have put my trust in his abilities."

The panic built up in Dane as he looked at the clock. The big hand was on the eight. Only seconds left. If the captain wasn't going to do anything, Dane would. Maybe he would run and try to tell Murdoch himself, make a break for the bridge, something, anything...

"But I do think I will have myself a look," Captain Smith said, and Dane saw that his face was filled with a doubt that hadn't been there just a moment before.

What had he seen?

Smith was walking purposefully toward the door when he stopped, and for a moment all three of them froze, listening.

Dane had once read a quote from one of the passengers when he had been doing research for his *Titanic* report at school. Mrs. Stuart J. White had felt the *Titanic* hit the iceberg and said it felt as if the ship had run over about a thousand marbles.

She was right. A slight bumping, a slight grinding.

The three of them stared at each other, motionless.

It was too late.

# CHAPTER EIGHTEEN

"It's happened," Dane muttered as he looked at Cliff and the captain, his eyes wide. His heart felt heavy, his stomach queasy and sick. He had failed. Failed to save the ship and its passengers, and now everyone would pay.

"That could be anything," the captain stated. "We might have thrown a blade—"

*Threw a blade?* Dane thought dismally. What a stupid saying. And no, they hadn't "thrown a blade." They had "hit an iceberg."

He remembered his history and what was to happen next. "It was an iceberg," he said. "You'll go out on the deck to see now."

The captain walked the rest of the way to the door and set the book down on a tiny table next to the door. "Of course I will," he said importantly, stiffening up a bit at being told by a boy what to do. "I'll be back in a moment. You two stay here." He then pulled the door shut behind him, leaving Cliff and Dane to stare at each other hopelessly.

"Well, that's it, is it?" Cliff questioned.

Dane walked in a daze to his chair and dropped into it. His legs felt rubbery and had lost what had remained of their strength. "I guess," he mumbled.

He felt numb with despair and fear. Would this nightmare never end? He had tumbled into this dream world, but how would he get out? Or would he get out? Dane lowered his head in his hands. He felt like crying.

"Well, I for one am not going to sit around here and wait to go down," Cliff said as he strode to the door. "I don't know what to do, but I won't be caught dead here."

Dane raised his head and caught Cliff's eye. Cliff, realizing what he said, cracked a smile.

"Did I just say that?"

Dane smiled back. "You did."

Cliff, sensing that some of the tension had been lifted, said, "Well, that was a real ice breaker, wasn't it?"

Dane couldn't contain himself. His fear and despair melted away as he burst out laughing at Cliff's second unintentional joke.

Cliff raised his eyebrows. "What—"

"Ice breaker," Dane gasped out. "We just hit an iceberg—" he stopped as another gust of laughter rolled over him.

"Oh, right," Cliff said as he got his own faux pas. He began to laugh as well despite their dire situation.

"That was bad!" Dane wheezed. "I had a sinking feeling about that one."

And then they were both roaring; Cliff was leaning against the doorway and Dane had fallen out of his chair and was rolling on the soft carpet. The seriousness of the moment had, at least for the moment, passed.

At last, gasping for breath, Dane picked himself up. "To business," he said. A glance at the table, with the lamp, revealed to him an extra watch that belonged to the captain. It wasn't a digital wristwatch with a light, of course, but a pocket watch with a chain. *Better than nothing*, he thought, as he removed his watch from his wrist and stuffed it in his pocket. In his opposite pocket he crammed Smith's watch. He was glad that the captain was a clock-watcher with more than one available timepiece. *Lucky for me*, Dane thought.

"What are you going to do?" Cliff said as he wiped away the tears of laughter from his eyes.

"Find my sister. And you?"

"Not sure. I was rather hoping it wouldn't come to this."

Dane sighed heavily. "Me too."

"Do you have any suggestions? I mean, you do seem to be the one who knows what's going on."

"Do I? I couldn't save the ship even though I had the

book."

"It's a big ship. There's a lot you can't control, eh?"

"But I should have been able to—"

Cliff held up his hand. "It's already the past now. The question for us is what to do now."

A flicker of light came on in Dane's head. He couldn't save the ship. Maybe he was not meant to save the ship. Could he really have been able to have that much power over something that was such a huge part of World history?

Maybe he couldn't save the ship, but he would try to save his sister, and…

"The bellboys."

Cliff brightened. "Yes. I saw in your book we all died. Do you think we can change what happens?"

Dane dashed for the door and grabbed the book as he went. "We're not going to know if we just sit here. I'm going to get my sister. You work on the bellboys. Try to get them on one of the first lifeboats. They were mostly empty." Dane cracked the door and peered out into the hall.

They were no passengers, but not for long. Soon this place would be like a Sunday afternoon at a Bronco's game.

"Will they let us on the lifeboats? Don't they traditionally board women and children first?" Cliff asked as he clicked the light off, a gesture that amused Dane. Here the ship was about to go down and they were conserving energy.

"Yes. It will be women and children first," Dane confirmed. "Officer Lightoller will even insist on boarding only women and children."

Cliff, now in the hall, threw up his hands in despair. "But these are children! Most of them are only a little older than you!"

"I know, but the officers will tell you that you are part of the ship's crew and that you will have to wait."

"The news just gets better and better, doesn't it?" Cliff muttered. "All right. I'll see what I can do."

"Better hurry," Dane said as he closed the captain's door. "There's no panic now, but there will be."

"Right," Cliff said. Then he stuck out his hand, which Dane shook solemnly. "Good luck."

"You, too," Dane said.

"See you on the…the what? The rescue ship."

"*Carpathia.*"

"Right. Well, here goes."

The two parted ways then, and as Dane began his way through the maze of corridors he hoped Cliff was right. He hoped they would meet on the Carpathia. It was unlikely, but there was still a little hope left.

By the time Dane reached the door of his sister's room he was flushed and out of breath. The book was still clutched tightly in his hand, ready to be used if needed. He wasn't sure what good it would do now; its time had come and gone. The proof that it could have yielded to unbelieving crewmembers was now locked inside its covers, useless. At this point none of them would care. Why would they want to read about their deaths when they could experience the real thing firsthand?

That thought depressed him even more.

Still, he carried it around, almost like a talisman. Its weight felt comforting somehow, like a friend. At the moment, it was his only friend. Even his watch had ceased to work.

Dane looked at the captain's gold watch. 12:12 A.M.

By now people would be stirring. There would be no cause for alarm yet, or so people would think. Only an indignation that stewards would awaken the rich over a thrown propeller blade or a lifeboat drill. But for those who did err on the side of caution and step into the lifeboats and row away from the ship, they would notice a slight lilt to the ship. Slight, but still there.

Thousands of gallons of water couldn't be wrong.

Dane rapped softly on the door, not wanting to alarm the girls. When no answer came, he knocked more insistently. The door opened a crack and Mrs. Arthur's face, gaunt and tired, peeked through.

"Dane?" she asked. "What time is it?"

"It's after twelve. I need to see my sister, if I may."

"It's after twelve, and you are still working?" Her eyes opened wider as she became more fully awake. "They are working you awfully—"

"Can I see my sister, ma'am?" Dane repeated, trying not to sound too panicked. "It's kind of an emergency."

"Emergency? What emergency?"

Dane tired of breaking the news gently. "There's been an accident. The ship hit an iceberg. I'd like to see Abby."

"Oh, my," Mrs. Arthur said, her hand flying to her throat. She pulled the door open and Dane entered, questioning what his next step should be.

His initial thought had been to save his sister. That had been his main mission, perhaps his whole reason for being sent here. But how could he leave all these people here, knowing full well where the ship was going to be in two hours?

Deciding he would grapple with that issue in a few moments, he waited for Mrs. Arthur to snap on the light.

"What should we do?" she inquired.

"Well, I'll tell my sister what is happening," Dane said as he approached Abby's bunk. "And then—"

He cut himself off and turned to Mrs. Arthur. "Where is she?"

Mrs. Arthur opened her eyes even wider. "She should be in bed!" she cried, dashing over to the empty upper bunk and gaping at it.

Dane's heart sank even further into his shoes.

"Great," he muttered.

# CHAPTER NINETEEN

Abby didn't know how long she had toured the immense ship, wandering up and down corridors, poking her nose into nooks and crannies, getting lost, softly calling her brother's name. It couldn't have been too long, but it felt like forever. She was red in the face, both from the exertion of walking the ship and from her tears. She had tried desperately to hold them in, to be strong, but with each passing moment and with each new dead end she could feel her fear mounting, her frustration growing. Tears had at last spilled over. She kept scrubbing them away, but they continued their constant downpour. If she didn't find Dane soon, she would have to worry about a lot more water than this.

She stopped, sighed, and leaned against the nearest wall. She didn't even know what floor she was on anymore.

Abby raised her stuffed bunny to her face. "I don't know what to do, Henry," she whimpered. She buried her face into the soft fur.

She was wiped out, tired, exhausted, out of ideas.

She had gone to bed at the same time as the other girls, which had been eight-thirty. "Sharp," as Mrs. Arthur would always say, whatever that meant. Mrs. Arthur had gotten ready for bed as well, having had a long and tiresome day chasing little girls. Filled with guilt, but doing it only because she needed to, Abby had gone to the small chair where Mrs. Arthur always kept her personal belongings at night and stolen the watch that Mrs. Arthur kept with her on a chain. She wished she had a watch like Dane's, one that lit up, but at the moment this was the best she could do.

Abby had crawled into bed, hiding the watch in her hand and then pulling her sleeve around it. Only when the lights had gone out had she let it slip out of her hand and onto the pillow.

Then the waiting had begun.

She wasn't going to go to sleep, she had decided. She was going to wait this thing out.

Abby had always enjoyed staying up late and had found it to be a personal honor when allowed to stay up past her normal bedtime. Waiting for her brother shouldn't be too hard, or so she had thought.

She had been wrong.

Staying up was only fun if there was something to do.

Having to sit alone in the dark, with no one to talk to, nothing to do, no TV, no CD player, was not her idea of fun. In fact, it was downright miserable. It hadn't been hard staying awake for the first fifteen minutes because of the excitement and novelty of what was going on. Who else would be able to brag of being on the *Titanic*? But the fascination had begun to die down by eight forty-five, and by nine-fifteen she was pinching herself, desperately trying to avoid sleep.

She pinched herself.

She slapped herself.

She composed songs in her head.

She did sit-ups.

She thought of at least fifty-two different names for Henry, her stuffed rabbit.

She hummed quietly.

She played finger games, cracked her knuckles, pulled on her toes, tugged at her hair, and bit her fingers.

Whew.

When had Dane said he would come? She had forgotten.

She remembered Dane had said that the ship would hit the iceberg by 11:40 P.M., so it would be some time before that that he would come to put her mind at ease. After he had rescued the ship, of course.

By eleven o'clock he hadn't arrived. The watch was hard to read in the dark; only a small shaft of light came in through the circular window. She could barely see, but there was enough light to observe that her brother, or hopefully brother to be, was late. He had said that he would come and get her before the accident, hadn't he?

She hoped so.

At 11:10 P.M. she was tired of waiting, so she slid out of bed and dressed. The deep breathing of those around her let her know that everyone was asleep. Grabbing her rabbit and Mrs. Arthur's watch she had let herself out the door, pulling it shut softly behind her.

She was alone. It felt strange.

The only time she had been by herself in the past couple of days was when she had gone to the bathroom. Other than that, everywhere she went, Mrs. Arthur and Abby's friends accompanied her. She had been escorted from place to place by the firm hand of Mrs. Arthur, who, like a mother hen, did not let the girls out of her sight. The fact that Abby had been able to sneak out into the hall alone was a miracle.

She had run over what seemed like most of the ship, although she knew it couldn't be since she kept running into locked gates. She hadn't seen many people, and when she had she ducked for the nearest cover or hallway, not wanting to be seen and reported. Twists and turns in the hallway lead her nowhere important. She kept an eye on the watch, becoming more frantic with each passing peek. Time was running out.

At last, 11:40 P.M., she had stood still and waited, staring at the watch. Deciding that it wasn't very safe, she had leaned against a door, grasping the doorknob to balance herself against the crash she knew was coming. That is if Dane had been unsuccessful.

What she eventually felt was a letdown in more ways than one. There was no huge crash like she had expected, just a slight rumbling sound and tickle underneath her shoes, almost unnoticeable. More importantly she knew now that Dane hadn't been able to save the ship.

Now it was 12:10 A.M., and still, no sign of Dane. She had only Henry to keep her company. Even the reassuring hum of the ship's engines had ceased. She leaned against the wall of wherever-she-was and sighed deeply, trying to stop the flow of tears and calm down.

Then her heart leapt.

Dane came down the hallway, walking toward her. She grinned as she prepared to run and hug him, but then her hopes plummeted again.

It wasn't Dane, but some other boy around the same age, maybe a little older.

The boy was wearing the same kind of uniform she had seen on Dane and looked like he was in a hurry. He didn't look very friendly and kept his eyes on the floor of the hall, walking fast. He probably knew about the crash and was getting people out of their rooms or something. She hated to bug him, but this was an emergency.

"Uh, can you help me?" she pleaded.

The boy stopped. "What do you want? I'm busy."

"I can't find my brother," Abby confessed.

The boy looked bored. "Sorry. I'm not a detective. What's his name?"

"Dane. He works with you, I think."

The change in the boy's face was incredible, immediate, and comforting. Abby felt sure he would help her now that he realized it was one of his workmates. His scowl became a smile as he bent down to her level.

"Dane? I know Dane. I bet you want to find him, don't you?" The boy held out his hand for her to take. "He's not down here, though. He's near the front of the ship."

Abby took his hand and the two began to walk. "Has there been an accident?" she inquired.

The boy glanced down at her. "Why yes, there has been. I was on my way to tell some passengers. But we'll find your brother first."

"You're nice," Abby grinned. "What's your name?"

"Roger," the boy replied.

After Dane and Mrs. Arthur had tossed the room in their frantic search for Abby and had not succeeded, Mrs. Arthur turned to him. He could hear the panic in her voice as she said, "Where has she gone?"

"Probably to find me."

"Why would she look for you so late at night?" She stared hard at him, her soft features beginning to harden in the glare of the overhead light. "You didn't tell her to, did you? Tell her to sneak out of the room?"

"No," Dane replied truthfully, hoping he didn't sound too defensive in the face of Mrs. Arthur's practiced stare. "I wanted to come and get her because of the accident."

"Oh," Mrs. Arthur replied, her look softening. *At least for now she believes me*, Dane thought.

Making a quick decision Dane said, "Let's get the girls up, Mrs. Arthur."

"Where are we going?"

"Let's get everyone on deck," he said. Already a plan was forming. The first boats left less than half full. Was there any way they could make it in time?

All he could do was try.

# CHAPTER TWENTY

"Lifeboat Seven leaves at 12:45 A.M. Capacity sixty-five. Occupants twenty-eight. Lifeboat Five leaves at 12:55 A.M. Capacity sixty-five. Occupants forty-one. Lifeboat Six leaves at 12:55 P.M. Capacity sixty-five. Occupants twenty-eight."

Dane's eyes scanned the lifeboat list in the *Titanic* book as his lips quietly mouthed the words. He gave the pocket watch a quick glance and saw that it was 12:50 A.M. Seven was gone, and Five and Six were about to be launched. His eyes slipped down the list, continuing to look for options for the trail of people who followed behind him, trying desperately to keep up with his long strides. His dark red clad legs were a blur.

He felt a bit like a mother duck must feel, leading her ducklings through danger to safety.

Behind him was Mrs. Arthur. She had two girls by

the hand, and the other three followed closely behind her. Behind them was Mr. Arthur, also holding the hands of two of the smaller boys. The rest of his charges trailed him at a close proximity, looking worried but no longer tired. The excitement of the moment had gotten the better of all of the orphans, who were trying their best to keep up with Dane.

Dane and Mrs. Arthur had wakened all of the girls and Dane had stood respectfully in the hall while Mrs. Arthur pulled them together and got them dressed. He had made continuous glances at his new watch, tapping his foot nervously as he watched time slip away as the water slipped in through a series of gashes that were the combined size of a twelve-foot square hole.

At last the girls joined him. Mrs. Arthur strongly suggested that they get Mr. Arthur and the boys, a suggestion he didn't argue with since he had thought about it while waiting in the hall. They began their trek to the front of the ship. The journey hadn't taken as long as Dane had thought it might; the girls were good under pressure and seemed to understand what was expected of them, even though they hadn't been told much about their dire predicament. It *did* take awhile, however, to locate Mr. Arthur and the boys, who they eventually found in the third-class saloon, looking slightly tired and bewildered. Mr. Arthur had gotten the boys up and dressed (and had even put on their lifebelts) after a steward had awoken them with the news that something was wrong. Dane was relieved they had found them when they did. A little longer, and Mr. Arthur might have wandered off with the boys, and then who knew how long it would take to meet up with them?

Then they had followed Dane's lead on their journey to the Boat Deck.

*"If only Mom and Dad could see me now,"* he thought. One moment school, football, church, video games. The next moment, changing history.

Life was funny.

Dane's eyes landed on Lifeboats One and Three in his book, which, according to his list, were launched at one o'clock. If they hurried, they might be able to make one of those. He picked up his pace even more, glancing behind him as he did. Instead of cries of protest from the children they quickened their pace as well.

Dane continued to switch his gaze from the hallways to the book to the map of the ship. The *Titanic* layout was beginning to come to him, so he didn't need the map quite as much as he had yesterday. When his eyes fell on the life-boat list to look for more options in case they missed Lifeboats One or Three, his attention was caught and held near the top of the list.

Something was happening.

At first he thought it was his eyesight blurring. He had

been up a long time, and been hit on the head, and this was more stressful than anyone could imagine. He fluttered his eyelids and stared harder, astonished.

It wasn't his eyesight.

Lifeboat Six, on the port side of the ship, had left with twenty-eight occupants. As he stared in amazement, the twenty-eight in bold black letters blurred, as if someone were dropping water on a child's watercolor painting. Then the inky blur began to draw back together. Dane gasped as the number twenty-eight changed to the number thirty-seven.

"More people just got on the lifeboat!" he yelled, elated. He wasn't sure what had just happened, but history had just been rerouted.

"What's that, Dane?" Mrs. Arthur wheezed behind him.

Dane turned to her. "I can do it!" he shouted at her, but not really to her. "I can change things!"

Mrs. Arthur smiled wanly. "That's nice, dear," she said.

Once on the sloping deck it didn't take Dane long to locate Lifeboat One. It was on the starboard side near the front of the ship. It was an emergency lifeboat, and with a quick flip of a few pages he discovered that first Officer Murdoch, the man who was in charge when the ship struck the iceberg, was manning the loading of the boat that originally had left with just twelve people.

"Mr. Murdoch," he said, resisting the temptation to tug on the busy man's sleeve.

"Yes," the sharply dressed officer said, glaring at Dane. When he saw it was a member of the ship's crew, he said, "Shouldn't you be off somewhere helping someone? Handing out lifebelts, perhaps? I'm extremely busy here."

"I *have* been helping, sir," Dane answered as sincerely as possible. "I have a group to put on the lifeboat. I see you don't have too many yet."

Murdoch looked over Dane's shoulder and saw the group standing there, looking cold and nervous in the brisk April air. "I suppose," he said. "But I prefer women and children only. The woman and children can get in, but—"

"But there's a man already in there!" Dane cried, pointing. He hated being a tattletale, but this was drastic.

"Please," Mrs. Arthur protested. "We're taking these children to America. I won't go if I can't be with my husband."

"Quite right!" the man in the boat said, standing. "Here here, Mr. Murdoch. I'll give this man my place!"

The woman sitting next to him grabbed his arm. "Cosmo!" she reprimanded.

Murdoch sighed wearily. "All right, all right," Murdoch grumbled. "You may sit down, Mr. Duff Gordon. They may all get in."

"But I'm not getting in," Mr. Arthur protested. "What about Abby? I must look for her!"

"I'll do it, sir," Dane said. "She *is* my sister."

"But that's not right," Mr. Arthur protested as Dane shoved him toward the boat already being loaded with Mrs. Arthur and the orphans. "I should be the one to stay."

"It's all right, sir. I'm not allowed in anyway. I'm crew," Dane argued gently.

Mr. Murdoch smiled proudly down at him. "You may get in if you wish," he said to Dane in a quiet, secretive voice. "There's room, and this one is ready to go."

"No," Dane said firmly as he watched Mr. Arthur resignedly step into the boat. "I have a sister on board and I have to find her."

Murdoch extended a hand. "Good luck, then," he said. And then, "Lower away!"

"Be careful, Dane!" Mr. Arthur hollered out to him. "Find her!"

"I will!" Dane shouted back. "I'll see you on the Carpathia!"

"Is she near?" Murdoch asked hopefully.

"Uh, I think so," Dane mumbled. Oops.

Mr. and Mrs. Arthur both waved to him, Mr. Arthur looking proud and Mrs. Arthur wiping away tears. He waved back as he grinned ear to ear. He couldn't help it.

He had done it!

Just to make sure, Dane opened the book and flipped a few pages until he found the lifeboat section. Sure enough, the letters had blurred. The ink pulled together as metal filings would to a magnet.

The number was now twenty-three.

"Yes!" Dane cried triumphantly. His grin, already big, broadened even more.

# CHAPTER TWENTY-ONE

Up until that moment Dane hadn't paid much attention to the condition of the ship. His attention had been focused on trying to keep his head on straight as he went about the business of saving his sister.

But now there was a lull in the activity as he stood in the cold, his breath passing out of him in fluffy white clouds. Now there was just a moment to look.

He was standing on the deck at a slight angle. Nothing major yet, but it was enough of a slant to realize there was no hope for the ship. Dane mused briefly that if the passengers on board were able to have the same view of the ship that the passengers in the lifeboats had, the panic on board would be much worse. As it stood right now, though, the panic hadn't yet begun to ripple through the crowd. Dane observed men, women, and children milling about on the deck, but he knew that it was only a short matter of time before the wandering and milling would become more purposeful. It would turn into an all out panic.

From overhead came a flash like lightning and a burst of sound as a white distress rocket shot off, bathing the ship in a bright glare. Some of the passengers and crew stopped to stare, including him. He figured it was probably one of the last rockets to be sent. It wouldn't do any good.

Suddenly Dane was shaken from his fireworks watching by Cliff, who came to a screeching halt so fast he knocked Dane to a knee.

"Sorry, old man!" Cliff said as he pulled Dane to his feet. "I was hoping I would find you here! Did you get your sister to a boat?"

"No," Dane sighed. "I haven't seen her yet. But I did get the others to a lifeboat."

Cliff pumped Dane's hand. "Good show!" he said excitedly. "I had some luck myself."

"The bellboys?"

"Yes!" Cliff said, the elation evident on his face. "How did you know?"

"The book told me. It changed." Cliff grinned broadly. "You're kidding!" he exclaimed.

Dane shook his head. "Nope. How did you save the bellboys?"

Cliff gave a wry, mischievous smile. "There are now a bunch of pretty ladies in Lifeboat Six."

Dane smiled as he thought about what that must look like. If only someone on the *Titanic* had had a camera…

"You'll have to fill me in on that later. Right now I have to find Abby. Why didn't you leave?"

"I'm crew. They probably wouldn't have let me on. Besides, I wanted to find you."

"Thanks," Dane said, genuinely touched. That someone would stick his own neck out for him was foreign and strange. His guilt for the way he had been treating his sister when they were in Colorado intensified. How could he have been such a jerk?

"I'll help you look. Where do we begin?" Cliff began enthusiastically. "Any ideas?"

Dane shrugged helplessly. "I don't know what to do—"

"There!" Cliff shouted. Dane followed his pointing finger to the entrance of the first-class stairway. He was just in time to see Roger spinning clumsily from the two of them with a surprised look on his face. He crashed through the door. Cliff sprang into action and began closing in on him as Dane followed.

"What's going on?" Dane called out after him.

"He looks guilty to me!" Cliff shouted back. "He saw us and started to run!"

The two burst through the door and charged down the Grand Staircase, hot on Roger's heels. Cliff's legs gave him the advantage over Roger and before long Cliff had corralled him by his uniform collar and was dragging him to the floor.

Dane looked nervously around him for people, wondering who was watching the accosting of one of the ship's help. But no one was gawking at the three boys. The area had been flushed of most of the crowd as the lure of watching the lifeboats pulled them away. The few people who were there were engaged in quiet conversation and weren't interested in watching this scene play out.

"What did you do with his sister?" Cliff demanded, kneeling on Roger and grabbing his uniform in his hands.

Roger coughed as his face turned red. "I have no reason to tell you," he choked out.

"I'll give you a reason," Cliff said as he slammed Roger on the multi-colored black and white tile. "How 'bout I split your head?"

"Go ahead and split my head," the large boy spat out. "I saw the book. We're all going to be dead in an hour anyway." He glared at Dane. "I owe you this one," he said, snarling. "I'll never tell you where your sister is."

Cliff glanced at Dane with a "What are we going to do now?" look.

Dane's watch said 1:31 A.M. There was less than an hour to go. He didn't have much time.

He dropped to his knees and began to thumb through the book. "Let him sit up," he said to Cliff. Cliff reluctantly relaxed his grip and Roger, with some struggling, sat up.

"Look," Dane said, holding open the book. "You see this? This is the lifeboat list. The number of people who got into this lifeboat has changed because Cliff here got them to a boat. I could tell you what boat to get on so you could escape if you tell me where my sister is."

"No!" Roger spat out resentfully. "I didn't look closely at that page anyhow. You could be lying."

A sudden idea hit Dane and he riffled through the book, not remembering what page he was searching for. At last he found the photograph of Cliff and the bellboys, the photograph he was not a part of because he had still been officially a passenger. In triumph he held the book out for Roger and Cliff to see.

"It says most of the bellboys live now! The other day it said that none of them survived! Cliff, you made a difference!" Dane could barely contain his excitement. His hands were shaking.

"Let me see that," Cliff asked, holding out his hand. He scanned the page. "The only two that did not survive were Cliff Harris, the captain of the bellboys, and Roger Carp."

"Don't you see?" Dane almost bellowed. "Before it said you all died. Now we only have to worry about the two of you!"

"What about you?" Cliff asked.

"I'm almost too nervous to look," Dane said as he took

the book from Cliff and searched it for the picture of him and his sister and the other orphans. Finding it, he looked at the photograph and then the caption. "Mr. and Mrs. George Arthur with their orphans on their way to America. All of them survived except for Abby and Dane Sheridan, a brother and sister who lost their life on the ship."

Dane groaned. It was so hard to read it in print.

"What does all this have to do with me?" Roger asked as he rubbed his head where Cliff had injured him.

Dane offered the book to Roger. "I'll trade you. This for showing me where Abby is."

Roger reached out tentatively as Dane continued. "You can use this to help yourself. Maybe you can find a lifeboat or something. It will give you some ideas—"

Roger snatched the book away from Dane and stared thickly at it, weighing his options. At last he stood, wobbling a bit. "I should have taken this while I had the chance."

"Where is she?" Dane demanded impatiently.

"The gymnasium," he said. "She's with the instructor, Mr. McCawley. I told him she was a lost passenger. He agreed to look after her."

"Show us," Cliff spat out, obviously not trusting a word Roger offered.

"Why? Big Clifford can't find his way to the gymnasium?"

Cliff grabbed the boy by the collar again and leaned in

close. "No, I just don't trust you."

"Let him go, Cliff. Let's just go look for her," Dane said, increasingly aware that time was of the essence.

"Yeah, let me go, Cliff," Roger sneered as he pulled himself from the older boy's grip. "I'll be going now, if you don't mind. I have other things to do rather than help you two."

"Like saving your own neck?" Cliff retorted.

Roger smiled. "Why not? I bet everybody will be doing that pretty soon."

"Come on," Dane urged Cliff, pulling at his sleeve. Together the two flew up the stairs, leaving Roger to stare after them.

"I hope he gets his," Cliff muttered.

After his two ex-coworkers had disappeared, Roger flipped open the prize that had been given him and located the lifeboat list. Seeing that he still had a few moments left to save himself, his mind quickly slipped to how he could liberate some of the jewels from the purser's office.

"A few minutes won't hurt," he said in a quiet voice, remembering the section he had read earlier about all of the valuables that had taken up residence on the bottom of the ocean. "This job doesn't pay much, anyway."

Dane and Cliff burst through the gymnasium doors

and immediately began to hunt for Abby. Dane pushed his way through the throng of passengers who were milling about, talking, testing the equipment, killing time. It didn't take him long to locate the burly man he recognized from photographs as the gym instructor, Mr. McCawley.

"Excuse me, sir. Did, uh, were you given a girl?" he stammered, feeling stupid.

"What?" the man asked as he turned away from a passenger he was instructing on the punching bag.

Dane shook his head, trying to rephrase. "Did a bellboy ask you to watch a lost girl? About this tall?" Dane held up his hand to approximate Abby's height.

"No, I think not," the man began, but that was enough for Dane.

"Cliff! She's not here!" he hollered out. Cliff, who had been checking the mechanical horses, rushed to his side.

"It figures," he snarled, rolling his eyes. "What now?"

Dane blinked away the tears of frustration that were threatening to spill out as he fought the urge to yell. He would have liked to punch one of the punching bags if it hadn't already been in use.

"It won't do us any good standing in here," he grumbled, and they exited and stood on the starboard side of the ship. Dane reached into the pocket holding his broken watch and retrieved it.

"Lot of good you did me," he said at it, then with a

mighty heave he threw it into the black water. Cliff watched silently and respectfully, not knowing what to say.

They turned and watched the ebb and flow of the crowd, and they gasped as they heard gunshots coming from farther back on the ship.

"It's getting bad," Dane commented.

"What's that noise?" Cliff asked as he cocked his head to one side.

"Officer Lowe's pistol," Dane answered. "Or Officer Lightoller. He's trying to protect—"

"No, not that. That! Listen!"

The crowd noise continued to escalate but Dane closed his eyes, tried to concentrate, tried to hear the sound Cliff was hearing. He fought his rising panic, willed himself to be calm and breathe slowly.

His eyes snapped open. "A bell?"

"Yes," Cliff replied. "Who would be ringing a bell? And where is there a bell, anyway? Meals are announced with a bugle. Do you remember anything about a bell in your book? Too bad we—"

"The crow's nest. What about the crow's nest?" Dane replied excitedly.

"He wouldn't have—" Cliff began.

The two looked at each other, and then pushed their way through the crowd to the front of the ship, towards the *Titanic's* sinking foremast.

# CHAPTER TWENTY-TWO

Dane and Cliff stood behind the rail of the Bridge and stared at the small girl in the crow's nest. Seeing that she had gotten their attention, she had ceased to ring the bell and was now waving excitedly to them. Dane could barely hear her small voice over the distance between them and the hiss of the oncoming water, which was now covering the forecastle deck and falling down the stairs.

"Oh, I can't believe anyone would do that," Cliff said as he stared, astonished, mouth wide open.

"I've got to go get her," Dane said to Cliff as he waved to Abby. She jumped up and down jubilantly, looking to Dane more like a small child awaiting an amusement park ride than someone on a sinking ship.

"Well, you can't go out to her like that! You'll be swept away! Wait here!"

Dane watched him walk up the sloping Boat Deck for

a moment before he turned his attention back to his sister. He cupped his hands to his mouth and yelled, "Hold on, Abby! I'm coming!" He wasn't sure if she heard him or not, but in any case she waved back to him.

He glanced at his watch. Almost two o'clock now. If memory served, he had about fifteen or twenty minutes left before the whole thing dropped out from underneath all of them. If he didn't hurry...

"Here. Look what I've found."

It was Cliff, who had returned with two lifebelts dangling from his hands. He dropped one on the floor and draped the second over Dane's shoulders and began to tie. "I hope you don't catch a bad case of pneumonia out there," he said.

"I hope I don't catch a bad case of death out there," Dane responded. "Thanks for the lifebelt, though, Cliff."

Cliff looked at Dane sheepishly. "I'd go with you, but I can't swim. In a pool I'm okay, but out there right now I'd be fish food. Even with a lifebelt."

"That's all right," Dane said. "Better find yourself one of them, just in case."

"Yeah. This one is for Abby. Good luck."

"Thanks," Dane said again as he took the lifebelt. "See you on the Carpathia, right?" he added hopefully.

Cliff grinned. "I'll do my best."

Dane watched him retreat for a second time and felt a

sadness sink into him he had never felt before. The chances of seeing Cliff again anywhere except in the deceased section of a *Titanic* history book were slim.

He clambered on top of the rail and looked down in the inky blackness and felt his legs go weak. It reminded him of the time his friend had dared him to go off the high dive at the pool. Instead of just jumping in he had allowed himself to be psyched out by the sheer drop into the clear water far below. He might have stayed up there forever if a friend hadn't given him a helpful shove.

He wished someone were here now to make him take the plunge. Right now, his legs just didn't want to obey and make him face the ice-cold water.

"Are you going to jump, son, or just stand there?" came a voice from below him. Dane, startled, almost fell off of the tilting rail. Steadying himself he glanced down and saw Captain Smith.

"Oh, it's you," the captain said as he pulled himself up next to Dane. "Where's your fancy book?"

"I loaned it to someone," Dane answered.

"Ah. It didn't do us much good anyhow, now did it?" Captain Smith questioned as he stood on the railing. He laid a hand on Dane's shoulder to steady himself.

"I guess not," Dane sighed. "All I've got now to help me get through this is my mind."

"That's all you need then anyhow, isn't it? C'mon, let's

jump this thing together."

And with that Captain Smith grabbed Dane's hand. "Be British, men!" he called out. "Every man for himself! Abandon ship!"

The two of them took the plunge.

From up in the crow's nest Abby sucked in her breath as she saw Dane jump in the ocean with the old man. She watched anxiously for his head to break the surface, her hands gripping the back of the big bucket she was standing in that was the crow's nest.

One second, two seconds, three seconds...

And then he was up, gasping for breath, whipping his head and snapping hair and water out of his face. Abby jumped up and down, squealing as she saw him kick towards her, holding the other life jacket in front of him like a kickboard. The old man Dane had jumped in with came to the surface and swam off back toward the sinking ship.

"Dane! Over here, Dane!" she cried out.

Dane kicked out harder, then stopped, afraid that as he neared the mast he would float right by it. He wrapped the extra life jacket around his neck, then reached out and grabbed the mast one handed. He reeled himself in, gasping.

"Dane! Are you okay?" she bellowed down to him.

"C-c-cold!" was the stuttered reply.

Abby could see that there was no way for Dane to

climb up to her. He would have to wait in the freezing water until the mast had sunk enough to reach her, and she didn't know how long that would be.

What could she do?

On the floor, pooled around her feet, was the rope that the mean boy Roger had tied her up with after he had tricked her into thinking that her brother was up here. She had been able to wriggle out of the ropes with only a little rope burn. Scooping up one of the ends, she tied it as tightly as she could to the mast.

"Dane! I'm going to throw you a rope, okay?"

Her brother nodded shakily. Even from up above she could tell he was as cold as an ice cube.

She tossed the rope down into the churning water. Luckily the rope was long enough to cover the closing distance between Dane and the lookout's perch. He grasped the rope, gave it a tug, and began to climb hand over hand, using his feet to help. The going was difficult at first as Dane forced his frigid muscles to cooperate, but quickly enough he felt them warming up to the task.

At last he tumbled into the nest, Abby straining and pulling at his lifejacket to help him out. He stood uneasily on jelly legs, shivering in the April air. Abby wrapped her arms around him in a big bear hug.

"I knew you'd come!" she said, ecstatic. "I knew you'd come!"

Dane hugged her back, hard. Through chattering teeth he said, "A-r-re y-y-ou o-okay?"

Abby nodded and held up Henry. "Henry is too," she said. "I was ringing the bell forever, and you came!"

"Yes, I did," Dane affirmed. He took the extra lifebelt and turned her around and began to strap it onto her, forcing his cumbersome, fumbling fingers to tie. "I wasn't getting on a boat until I found you," he said.

"I knew you wouldn't," Abby replied confidently. "Would you have gotten on one a few days ago?"

Dane felt sheepish at the bluntness of the question, and even more sheepish at the bluntness of the answer he knew was coming. "I guess I would have, maybe. I would like to say no, that I would have come after you anyway."

He completed the tying and turned her around to face him. "I'm sorry, Abby. I don't know what else to say. I was being selfish and wanted the house to myself, I guess."

Abby nodded as she took this in. She hugged him again, tight, dripping lifebelt to dripping lifebelt. "I forgive you," she said. "Even if we die here, I forgive you."

Dane breathed a sigh of relief as the heavy weight of guilt was lifted from him. He placed his hands on her shoulders and said, "Well, let's make sure we don't die, okay?"

"Okay!" she grinned. "What are we going to do now?"

Dane peered over the edge of the crow's nest at the ever-approaching water, trying to judge how much time they had before they were overcome with ice water. They didn't have that much time. Should they jump?

"Better stuff Henry into your lifebelt," he said. "I don't think he can swim."

"That's not what I meant, silly," Abby said as she followed Dane's orders. "I meant, should we wait or jump in?"

Dane groaned with confusion. He felt like a mouse trapped in a corner with the cat nearby, ready to pounce. "I wish…"

"You wish what?"

Dane glanced at the ship that was vanishing like the world's biggest magician's trick. His mind raced. He wished what? That this wasn't happening? That he could see the lifeboats more clearly in the dark and see which ones were full and which ones weren't? That he still had the book and would know what was going to happen next?

Yes.

"I wish I knew what to do now," Dane said to Abby. He looked down at her, saw her smiling back up at him, no doubt in her small face.

"You'll figure something out," she replied.

Maybe, Dane thought. But the principal said this was a game, and every game had to have a winner and a loser, right? And what if he were the loser?

He set his jaw determinedly. He wasn't a loser, and he wasn't going to lose this game. Looking down into her face again he was filled with self-confidence. Her face told him she had faith in him. Not in the situation, but in him. He wouldn't fail her.

"And I won't," he muttered. "I won't."

"What?"

"Fail," he told her.

"I know."

Straining his eyes into the darkness, dimly lit by the ship's lights, searching for an answer, he saw the frightening sight laid out before them. The ship's stern was raising itself high into the air with swarms of people massing their way towards the sky. More people were jumping off the temporary safety of the ship into the icy water so as not to be sucked under when it went down. And over on the port side of the *Titanic* Dane could see a boat, Collapsible B, he thought, being washed off of the Boat Deck with men struggling to stay on it.

"That's where we're going to swim," Dane said to Abby, pointing. "It's not too far—"

He was cut off by a creaking, groaning sound. He looked over to the forward funnel, which was leaning ominously in their direction as the front of the ship started its plunge.

And then he remembered.

"Abby, we have to get out of here now!" he shouted, his breath pouring out before him harshly. "The smokestack is going to collapse!"

"Is it going to land on us?" Abby asked, her eyes growing large.

"We're not going to wait to find out! Let's go!"

Dane pulled himself up onto the edge of the crow's nest, and then hauled Abby up beside him. The water was only a foot below them and closing in rapidly.

"Do you see that boat?" Dane asked her, pointing to Collapsible B. "That's the one we are going for. Can you swim?"

Abby nodded, gulping, clutching Dane's hand. From above they heard a snap, then a sound like a whip cracking through the air, then a splash. The wires holding the funnel upright was snapping. The smokestack was getting ready to fall.

Dane gripped his sister's hand tightly. "Jump!" he yelled.

# CHAPTER TWENTY-THREE

Roger burst out of a grotesquely tilting door; his bulky frame made more awkward by the barely concealed money and jewels threatening to burst out of his uniform. In his hand he held a canvas bag, also filled to bursting. His small eyes darted this way and that, looking for choices, the *Titanic* book still clutched in his damp hand.

"Where's Collapsible A?" he muttered as he began to move in the direction the book indicated. He hadn't had to learn the placement of the lifeboats when he had undertaken his brief training as part of the *Titanic's* crew (why would he on an unsinkable ship?) and now he was paying for it. He had taken more time than he had planned on, stuffing every pocket and sock and sleeve with valuables. He had planned on taking Lifeboat Four, but now he was too late for that. Collapsible A would have to be the answer.

He struggled on his way to the boat, lugging his heavy bag and trying to maintain his hold on Dane's book at the same time. He caught sight of Collapsible A half sunk in the water with a number of people pushing their way onto it. He neared the boat, ready to ask the nearest crewmember for some help, when his way was blocked.

"Hello, Roger," Cliff said.

Roger cowered as if he had been struck. "Out of my way, Clifford," he bleated, hating the way his voice sounded, weak and petulant.

"Or what?" Cliff inquired. "You'll tie someone else to the crow's nest?"

Roger grimaced, his face a mask of uneasy wariness in the dim light of the *Titanic's* deck lights. "I didn't—" he began.

"Don't even try to lie," Cliff snapped angrily as he snatched the bag away from Roger. "Let me guess. More stolen property?"

"Give that back!" Roger cried desperately as he dropped the book and reached to retrieve his loot.

"It doesn't belong to you, Roger," Cliff said calmly. Then with a gleam in his eye, he added, "but let's see what it means to you." And using an underhand toss, Cliff pitched the bag down the slanting deck and watched it as the ship's light tracked its noisy trail down the steeply sloping deck.

"No!" Roger shouted. He turned from Cliff and chased

the bag the short distance to where it had struck the water, his arms flailing wildly to help him keep his balance.

Cliff watched as Roger stumbled into another passenger heading the other way up the deck, fell, and landed head first into the water at the point where his bag had vanished. He continued to gaze at the spot, waiting for the boy to reappear.

The seconds stretched, seemingly forever.

At last Cliff said, more to himself than anyone else, "Well, I guess he made his choice."

"Does someone have a knife? We need to cut the boat free from the ship!" Cliff heard someone yell from behind him on the swamped lifeboat. He felt in his pocket, found a pocketknife, and hurried to Collapsible A.

Dane had been to water parks before and had always enjoyed the man-made waves striking him, letting himself be carried away by them. But when the first funnel let go of its moorings and crashed into the water with a deafening roar, it created a wave that was unlike anything he had ever felt before.

Before it had fallen, he and Abby had been gasping and struggling their way to Collapsible B (which had overturned and was being fought over by various passengers) and had been running out of steam. Dane could feel the freezing water sap his strength and he had sensed the same in Abby. Her enthusiasm was now replaced by overwhelming fatigue. Collapsible B, which really wasn't that far away, appeared to be retreating further from the ship.

When Dane heard the crumpling sound of the forward funnel (sounding as if God were crushing the world's biggest Coke can) he reached out and grabbed for Abby's lifebelt, but missed. "The smokestack's going to fall!" he called out. "Hold onto my hand!"

She reached for him, missed, tried again, and caught hold of his hand. He began to tell her not to look, not to watch as all of the passengers floundering underneath the massive funnel were crushed, but was cut short as the tower of metal gave the water a mighty whack like the crack of thunder. He and Abby were scooped up and were now riding a wave to their destination.

Only this water park had no lifeguards.

"Don't let go!" he shouted to her, but even as he did their grip on each other slipped and he watched in horror as she was torn away from him, screaming.

At last the wave subsided and he was near Collapsible B, but Abby was nowhere in sight. He thrashed around in the twenty-eight degree water, seeing and hearing all of the passengers yelling for lifeboats to come back, but no Abby.

"Abby! Where are you?" he called. Frigid saltwater

splashed into his mouth and raced down his throat. He gagged and spit, feeling the salt burn his lungs.

But the only sound to return to him was the passengers and the ship, in the final moments of its death.

"Abby!" he screamed. "Where—"

"We wouldn't want a fine lad like you in there, now would we?" said a voice close to his ear, and before he knew it strong hands had grabbed his lifebelt and given a mighty tug. He was now sitting on top of Collapsible B, sputtering and coughing.

"Where's my sister?" he asked the wet but otherwise neatly dressed man sitting next to him who had hauled him up. Dane thought briefly how well the man was dressed to drown. Under other circumstances it might have been funny.

"I didn't see any young people other than you," the man answered back. "Just a lot of these devils trying to pull us off." He held out his hand to Dane, a gesture Dane found both endearing and ridiculous all at the same time, given the circumstances. "I'm Colonel Gracie, at your service."

Dane absentmindedly shook the man's hand, but his eyes confirmed what the Colonel had said. Dane watched the game of king of the hill being played on the lifeboat. Men in the water were scrambling to get on the capsized boat, and men already on it were trying their best to push them off. Dane looked out at the dark water, black as an oil slick, trying to spot the face of his sister. But all he could see was a mass of adult faces, and—

"Captain Smith?" he said as he saw the man's shaggy face. He seemed to be holding someone, dragging someone to the collapsible. It looked like it was hard work because the captain was not wearing a lifebelt, but he was making progress.

The captain drew near the boat and Dane's heart jumped as he recognized who the captain was holding.

Abby.

"Do you have room for one more, gentleman?" the captain asked. Dane lay flat on his stomach and held out his hands, and Captain Smith handed him the small lump that was his sister.

"Will you save yourself, sir?" a man asked, and even in the dark Dane could recognize the face of Officer Lightoller. But wordlessly the captain turned back to the ship and paddled away, his hatless head fading in the star-filled evening.

Dane sat up and tried to mold his body around his sister's still form. He rocked back and forth on the boat, gently shaking her.

"Abby?" he whispered softly, then shook her harder. His eyes filled with tears but he didn't make any attempt to scrub them away. He was dimly aware that the men he shared the boat with were frantically rowing with their hands, trying to escape the suction they thought was coming.

"Abby?" he asked again, sniffling. Tears from his eyes landed on her already soaked head.

He looked up as the lights on the ship flickered, then were snuffed out. He heard a tearing noise, then a crack, followed by a roar. In the pale light of the stars he watched as the ship split noisily into two pieces from all of the water weight that the ship had taken on. The back half slammed back into the water and the front half was sucked into the ocean. Shards of wood, metal and glass rained all around them like bullets.

Abby's eyes opened at the cavalcade of sound, as if awaking from a long sleep. "Dane?" she asked. "Was it a dream?"

Dane laughed and cried with thankfulness as he watched the back half of the ship rise towards the sky. "I don't think so," he said, shielding her eyes so she wouldn't see. The ship hovered in the air for a couple of minutes (which seemed to go on forever to Dane), completely vertical, before going down slowly, like an elevator, rotating a bit as it descended. Finally it was over, with no sound but the cries of help.

The *Titanic* was gone.

Dane shifted his weight uncomfortably on the bottom of the boat. The hard wood was so... so...

Soft?

Shivering with the cold, Dane gave a look at the boat he and his sister were planted on. He made a sound of wonderment at what he saw. Beneath him, instead of the stark white of the boat, was his colorful NFL bedspread.

"What?" he was finally able to gasp out in astonishment. His eyes shot up to the starry sky, but the bright stars shining overhead had been replaced with the white of the plaster above his bed. And quarterback John Elway was now taped to the wall in the spot where hundreds of people had been thrashing about only a moment before.

He squeezed Abby to tell her they were home, but when he looked into his arms Abby had disappeared.

He was now clutching empty air.

# CHAPTER TWENTY-FOUR

Dane blinked heavily, feeling as if he had just been awakened from a month-long sleep with a trumpet and a drum. His eyes took in the room with its posters, models, and desk. He looked at what he was wearing; white T-shirt, jeans, Nikes. The same stuff he had been wearing when he had left. Lightning still flashed across the sky as thunder rumbled, and Zelda, his dog, still jumped nervously as she looked at the rain tapping against the window.

How long had he been gone?

He looked at his watch, only to discover his arm was bare. On a hunch he dug into his pocket and found the captain's pocket watch, gleaming and gold in the glare of the overhead lights and looking as out of place here as his watch had looked on the *Titanic*.

It was 6:28 P.M. Dane sucked in his breath. Could it be that his two-day trip had taken no time at all? Had indeed worked in reverse? It was now before dinnertime on the day he had been thrust back in time.

And what about Abby?

Dane dropped the watch and leapt up and charged for the door, his heart racing. He flew down the stairs; his feet carrying him down so fast he almost went head over heels. Hearing sounds coming from the kitchen Dane bolted for the doorway.

"Mom!" he shouted as he neared the kitchen door. "Where's—"

Suddenly something flew at Dane and hit him hard in the midsection, taking his breath away in a whoosh.

"Dane!" Abby virtually screamed as she wrapped herself around him tightly, as if she hadn't seen him in years.

Dane laughed inwardly at the thought.

Lifting her off the ground he gave her a hug that would make a bear proud. "How are you?" he asked, smiling from ear to ear.

Abby whispered to him conspiratorially. "You were holding me on that boat and then I was here in the kitchen. I think I was helping Mom get dinner ready."

"I was upstairs on my bed when you left," he whispered back. "I was afraid you wouldn't be here."

Abby hugged him again as Dane's mom came and leaned against the doorjamb, a tomato and knife in her hands.

"I'm glad you came for me," Abby said quietly, her eyes large and thankful and sincere.

"Any time," he said back.

Dane's mom, feeling like she had missed something, said, "What's going on, you two?"

"Nothing," they both said at once.

It didn't take long the next day for Dane's name to be called on the school's intercom.

"Mrs. Magruder, would you please send Dane Sheridan to the office?"

There were a few quiet catcalls as Dane stood and walked across the room to the door, his legs shaking only slightly.

Once in the school office he was ushered into the principal's office.

"Ah, Dane. Good to see you. Please have a seat," Mr. Hill said, waving to a chair. Dane sat obediently, his stomach tied up in knots even though he figured he probably wasn't in trouble anymore. There was just something about being called to the principal's office that did that to one's stomach no matter what it was about.

Mr. Hill had a seat and folded his hands together on his desk and stared hard but not unkindly at Dane. "So, what did you think?"

"Sir?" Dane asked, not sure what to say.

The principal smiled. "If nothing else you learned some manners. I mean, what did you think of your little game?"

*Little?* Dane thought. The game had been as little as the *Titanic* itself.

"It was good," he said, which sounded simple and stupid at the same time.

Mr. Hill pushed on. "I assumed you learned something about yourself?"

Dane thought hard. Of course he had. If anything, he felt better about himself than he ever had in his entire life. He realized that when pushed up against a wall he would fight for himself and anyone he cared about. It hadn't taken him long, either, to find out how much he had cared for his foster sister. He had cared enough to risk his own life when he could have easily escaped harm's way.

The principal smiled, as if reading Dane's thoughts. "You really don't need to tell me all about it. I know what happened."

"How?" Dane questioned.

Mr. Hill avoided a direct answer to the question. "Another story for another time. Do you feel you won the game?"

"I wasn't told the objective right away, but if it was to

save my sister, then I guess I did."

"Sister? Not Abby? Not 'some girl?'"

Dane grinned, a little sheepishly. "We decided last night as a family to take her in. Permanently."

Mr. Hill smiled. "And I'm sure your change in attitude had something to do with the decision?"

Dane nodded and smiled back. "Yeah."

"You asked how I knew how you did," Mr. Hill said as he pulled open a desk drawer. "You might be interested in this."

Dane leaned forward in his chair and looked at the object the principal had put on his desk. It was a large paperback, but wrinkled and warped. *The Life and Death of the Titanic: Disaster on a Grand Scale* it said on the cover.

"The book—" Dane began.

"Yes, the book. It was on my desk this morning. I compliment you."

"Can I see it?" Dane asked eagerly.

"No, but I'll do one better," the principal said. "When games are played the winner often gets a prize, right?" He pushed the book across the desk to Dane. "It's yours."

"Really?" Dane asked, hardly able to conceal his excitement as he jumped up and snatched the volume.

Mr. Hill gave him a broad smile. "Happy reading."

Dane was sent back to class and put the book in his desk where it sat the whole morning, calling to him, begging to be read. Dane felt like he had shut up an old friend in the dark.

After what seemed like an eternity Mrs. Magruder dismissed them to lunch and recess. Dane gobbled his food without tasting it, then dashed out to the playground when dismissed, the book clutched to his side. He found a shaded part of the playground underneath a tree and sat down, his back against the rough bark.

Fighting the urge to skip immediately to the section on survivors, Dane opened the book at page one and began to scan the pages, lest he miss something important.

It didn't take long to find a couple things of interest he knew hadn't been there before.

Like the letter written to one Mrs. Margaret Brown of Denver, thanking her for her courage on the lifeboats. The letter had been written by one of the ship's bellboys, a certain Dane Sheridan, who had wanted to commend her by letter for her bravery. The letter was under glass at the Molly Brown House in Denver. Dane decided someday he would have to go pay it a visit. It looked like it had been handwritten, *and* was in his handwriting.

There were some photographs of personal articles that had belonged to passengers. Also, there were some shoes, toys, glasses, and one article in particular that had stumped some researchers. It was a broken, but otherwise intact, black digital watch, now on display at a museum in Southampton.

Dane grinned as at last he reached the section on survivors, listening to the warped and water damaged pages crackle as he turned them. His eyes scanned the pages. They fell on a photograph of bellboys on the deck of the Carpathia, and his heart leapt as he read the caption under his breath.

"*Titanic's* bellboys. All of them survived except for Roger Carp from Portsmouth, England, who went treasure hunting in the purser's office and who was last seen by Mr. Clifford Harris, chasing a bag of money down the sloping deck after the captain of the bellboys took it from him and threw it in the water."

Dane stared at the caption. "What did you do, Cliff?" he muttered, but he thought he knew. Cliff had met up somehow with Roger and had forced Roger to make a hard choice.

"Poor Roger," he mumbled, shaking his head. He almost felt sorry for him.

He read on, a smile beginning to form on his face and growing as he continued his scanning and reading.

"Mr. and Mrs. George Arthur were among some of the third-class passengers to escape. Here they are shown on the *Carpathia* with their group of orphans, all of whom were successfully adopted."

Dane's grin broadened. "I wonder who took us in."

He flipped some more.

There was a painting of Captain Smith in the ocean, handing a small child to a boy on the top of an overturned lifeboat.

"Doesn't even look like me. My hair's not that dark," he muttered.

Another drawing showed Captain Smith standing on a rail of the ship getting ready to jump in, a boy by his side holding a lifebelt.

A drawing of a nameless boy and girl in the crow's nest of the sinking ship.

A photograph of all of the bellboys, Cliff and Dane included, standing in New York City with the Statue of Liberty behind them.

There was one of Cliff and Dane standing next to each other on the *Carpathia*. Cliff's feet were wrapped in bandages from the frostbite he had received while standing in the freezing water of Collapsible A, but other than that, he looked intact. Their arms were folded across their chests as they stood next to each other, their faces serious but their eyes full of life and mischief.

The last photograph Dane found of interest was one of a boy and a girl on the deck of the *Carpathia*. The boy was wearing a bellboy uniform and was bent over, giving the younger girl a piggyback. Both had broad smiles on their faces and looked as if the photographer had captured them in mid-play.

Dane touched the photo and smiled as he read the caption. "Two of Mr. and Mrs. Arthur's nameless orphans frolic on the deck of *Carpathia*."

Someone playfully kicking at his feet interrupted his reading. "Hey, Dane!" Abby teased.

Dane looked up. "Hi!" he said, genuinely pleased to see her.

"Give me a piggyback?" she asked, still chewing her sandwich from lunch.

"Sure," Dane said. He closed the book. His game was over; his task completed, his lesson learned, his game successfully won. He placed the book near his lunch sack and bent down so Abby could hop on his back. She did, and Dane galloped off across the playground with her whooping joyfully in the early afternoon sun.

## Mike Warner

has had a lifelong fascination with the Titanic, and insists that if he can't go see the ship in person, at least he can write about it. When he's not coaching his kids' soccer teams he can be found teaching fourth grade. He and his wife Ann live with their three children, Christopher, Samantha, and Jesse, in Centennial, Colorado. Included in their household is a small Lhasa Apso, named Rocky, that lets them live with him.

## Frank Ordaz

can't remember a time when he wasn't drawing something or someone. When he was seven, his father started exhibiting his drawings in local art shows in San Gabriel, California. By the time Frank was in high school he had already chosen the path of an artist as a career.

He graduated from the Art Center College of Design in 1980 majoring in illustration. Shortly thereafter he relocated to northern California and began painting for George Lucas's Industrial Light and Magic where he worked on such academy award winning films as *E.T.*, *Return of the Jedi* and *Indiana Jones and the Temple of Doom*. In 2006, Frank was commissioned by Laura Bush to paint the artwork for the annual White House Easter Egg Roll.

CPSIA information can be obtained at www.ICGtesting.com
Printed in the USA
BVOW11s1029220715

409894BV00016B/101/P